Buzzard's Roost

Megan Day

God Bless
+ Enjoy.
Megan Day

PublishAmerica
Baltimore

Isaiah 41:10

ISBN: 1-4241-4388-8
PUBLISHED BY PUBLISHAMERICA, LLLP
www.publishamerica.com
Baltimore

Printed in the United States of America

I would like to dedicate this book to my family who has always believed in me and gave me the courage to believe in myself. Especially to my Mom, Dad, Grandma and Grandpa Love who cultivated my desire to write and inspired me to follow my heart.

Special thanks to my husband, John, who gave me the opportunity to pursue my dream of writing. Without his indulgence and patience this novel would never have been completed.

Chapter 1

Her eyes fluttered open and darkness stared her in the face. Kristian slowly closed them again, took a deep breath, and tried again. One eyelid up, the other scrunched tight, she slowly moved her eye its entire circumference. Nothing but blackness greeted her. The damp air clung to her lashes and sent a chill down her spine

Shaking her head, she attempted to raise herself up. Bracing her elbows in the mud, she pushed until her head came off the ground. She no more got up and her shoulder collapsed. Squinting her eyes against the pain, she settled back to watch fuzzy spots flit behind her eyelids. Disgusted, she raised her arm to brush her hair out of her face. Not like it mattered, she couldn't see anything anyway.

Slowly, Kristian took mental inventory of her extremities. All the muscles felt battered, like she'd just gone ten rounds with Godzilla. Taking a deep breath, she let her mind wander over the individual pains. Her arms were aching and usable, but her legs were out of commission. When she tried to lift her thighs, the muscles refused to respond. Her mind said they should be lifting, but the heaviness in her knees told her they weren't. If it was any consolation, her toes on the right side still wiggled. Letting out a sigh, she became aware of a pounding in her head. It made the backs of her eyes throb and her ears ache.

Disoriented, Kristian strained to remember what happened. She'd left work early to take an afternoon jog through the hills. The sunlight and early spring air made it too tempting to stay indoors. Her job was beginning to stress her out, and a few quiet moments running always tended to ease her mind. Especially on such a beautiful day. Spring had touched the trees, and the green was astounding. Flowers were just starting to open up which added a kiss of color to last year's bed of leaves. A gentle breeze kept the warming air from being to hot. All the conditions were perfect for a run.

Kristian left her car in a gravel parking area and set out on her usual path. Since the garden club finished making trails through the wilderness preserve, she spent a lot of her alone time exploring the woods.

She'd rounded a bend by the creek concentrating on not thinking about her latest case. In her time doing social work, she'd dealt with her fair share of tyrannical husbands. She focused on helping the wives separate themselves from abusive relationships. This particular abuser frustrated every effort she made to get Cindy out. His temper hit too close to home for her to feel comfortable.

Something made her turn around, but…what was it? Think, girl, think. The creek was gurgling and a slight breeze stirred the grasses. A noise, something out of place, something that made her feel like she was being watched. The creepy shivers ran down her spine and hairs on her arm stood at attention, as she tried to brush it off.

Kristian gasped. Him. He had found her. Again. Running… slippery rocks…falling, falling…a blow to the head and then…nothing.

Panic set in, as her chest constricted. Her lungs were tightening and her breath came in labored wheezes. *Oh God, help me now*, she inwardly prayed. The all encompassing darkness was making her head spin. Absolute darkness. It just registered that she couldn't see anything. Why was it so blasted dark? Gulp...what if the darkness wasn't really darkness? What if...what if she was...blind? She'd read where a blow to the head could do that.

Kristian whirled her head around to see if she could catch a flicker of light. Anything to alleviate the void. *Fear thou not for I am with thee*...Her favorite verse flickered through her mind, but it couldn't calm her nerves. It carried with it too many memories of past fears to do her any good. She swallowed hard. Remnants of the past floated like holographs before her eyes and made her heart beat faster. Could he be watching?

Stiffening her spine, Kristian instinctively recoiled. He was probably ogling her with those penetrating eyes. Cobalt blue with a hint of hatred to make them seem darker. She tried to assume the fetal position, but her legs still wouldn't cooperate. The bastard was probably enjoying his handy work with that know it all grin. Watching her squirm was something he had turned into an art form. He always loved to strip her of her sanity. Picking and prodding until all rational thought was impossible. He had an unbelievable gift for controlling her from the inside out.

"Stop it!" Kristian shouted. The sound of her voice echoed off invisible walls. As it slammed against her senses, she willed herself to pull it together. She couldn't let the past and who she was then keep her from overcoming now.

From the sound of it, she was enclosed in some sort of cave. It couldn't be all that big the way her voice bounced around.

"Why???" Kristian screamed in rage. Anger was beginning to take over her earlier queasiness.

Why…why…why came back as her only answer. Just when she was starting to make a life for herself and Caleb, he had to come crawling out of her past to destroy everything. Years of hiding and working to separate herself from him meant nothing. She'd finally let her guard down and stopped looking over her shoulder or jumping at every shadow. Even though she swore she'd never open up to a man again, she found herself telling her secrets to someone she actually intended to marry.

Kristen smiled in spite of herself. It wasn't like Austin had really given her much choice. He'd shown up at a time when she really needed a friend and had soon grown into a soul mate. His genuine kindness and rugged charm touched her heart in a way she never dreamed possible. She tried to resist, but he was so great with Caleb.

Tears slid unbidden down her cheeks. Poor Caleb. She'd wanted to protect him from this.

Chapter 2

Cowboy hat cocked to the side, he rounded the table. His gait bespoke purpose, as he sauntered to the middle of the room. Six shooters hung slightly below the hip and his jeans were migrating south. Batman underoos peeped out the top just below the disheveled shirttail.

"Dis water hole ain't big enough for the both of us," Caleb drawled in his best Woody voice. The movie of the week was Toystory, and he loved to be the drawstring cowboy.

"To 'finity and beyond!" he shouted as he pulled both guns out. His pants dipped dangerously close to the floor, and his rival didn't look too impressed.

Rascal lay haphazardly beside his water bowl, tongue lolling to one side. The most action he'd seen all day was watching a fly buzzing out the window. He wasn't about to get motivated now.

"Your 'posed ta run! How are you going to be the bad guy if you don't even move when I try to shoot you?"

The lab rolled over and thumped his tail slightly. Maybe, if he played along, the kid would be quiet and scratch his belly.

"Hello!" Caleb yelled. His voice dripped four year old

exasperation. "You don't die till I pull the trigger! Don't you pay attention to nothing? How my 'posed to 'prastice' my cowboy with you doing it all wrong. Golly!"

With that, the boy plopped down on the floor shaking his head in disgust. What was the world coming to when the bad guys quit doing what they were supposed to?

Rascal looked at him with his watery brown eyes. He seemed oblivious to the frustration he was causing. Slobber was dangling from the corner of his mouth, and he let out a sigh. The saliva dripped to the floor and joined the pool of others that had come before.

Caleb sat sulking. No one ever wanted to do what he wanted to do. The cat always ran from him, his frogs wouldn't stay in his pocket and his turtle refused to race in his sand box. He'd spent all day making that track out of water and sludge. All he'd managed to do was get his butt paddled for tracking mud in the house.

A slow grin spread across his face. It sparked the dimple in his cheek, and his blue eyes started to dance. Jumping to his feet, Caleb knew how he was going to handle the situation. He'd seen his mom do it a zillion times whenever he opted not to listen.

Standing to his full height, he put both hands on his hips. He cleared his throat for effect and commanded,

"Do you need to 'cwean' your ears out, young man? If you don't start listening, you're going to be in big trouble, mister!"

Caleb nodded his head and waited for the magic to start. When his Mom said mister, he usually perked up and started minding his business. Momma didn't get upset that often, but she sure could motivate when she did.

The dog didn't move. Not a tail or even an ear was raised. Rascal didn't even have the sense to act ashamed of himself.

Rule number one when you were in trouble was to pretend like you were real sorry. Even if you weren't and didn't understand what the fuss was about. More tiny heiney's were saved by being contrite than by being bull headed.

Caleb let out a big breath real slow. In through the nose and out through flared nostrils.

"One…"

Nothing from the dog.

"Two…"

Still nothing. By this time with is Mom, Caleb was usually jumping into action. Obviously, Rascal wasn't too bright. Didn't the mangy mutt know if he had to call three, bad things were going to happen? Real bad. So bad that only one kid had ever let it go that far. Tyler from down the road said that he used to have a baby brother. One day, his Mom had to call three and she strung him up by his toes. By the time she was done with him, they had to trade him in for a pony. Tyler knows, too. He was five and knew just about everything.

"Don't make me do it, Rascal. Don't ya do it. I don't wanna have to say the three word, but I will if you don't start moving!"

Rascal rolled back on his belly and had the nerve to shut his eyes. He closed them lazily and started scratching his side with his hind leg. A nap sounded good about now. All that kid's yappin' had made him tired.

"Three!!" Caleb yelled. Nothing. Great, Caleb fumed. Now he was going to have to string up his dog and trade him in for a pony. What a rip! Oh well, at least he'd have something to ride when he was playing cowboy. That would be way better than sitting around arguing with a smelly ole dog any day.

He marched into the living room and grabbed his green jump rope. Caleb had never strung anything by its toes before. *Wonder if Rascal has toes,* he thought to himself. Oh well, if he didn't he could just tie his legs together and call it good.

"Caleb Michael Henry! What in creation are you doing?"

Caleb nearly jumped out of his skin. He was straddling Rascal and had his rope wrapped around three of his legs. Gretchen's voice made him drop everything.

"Are you tormenting that poor dog again after your mother told you not to?" Gretchen shifted her ample weight and started massaging her forehead with her thumb. "Answer me!"

Several strands of graying hair flirted with the creases around her eyes. She had a blue apron over her gingham dress and had most of her hair pulled back in a severe bun. Years of working outdoors had given her a rugged complexion, but her warm green eyes let you know her heart was still soft.

The boy stumbled, as he tried to step away from the dog. His foot caught on Rascal's tail, and he fell to the floor at Gretchen's feet. He went to stand up, and his boots caught on the cuff of his pants. Caleb went up, but the jeans went down leaving Batman exposed to the world. To his credit, he didn't even bat an eye. In one fluid motion, he scooped his pants up with one hand and straightened the six shooters with the other. With his tiny frame, he had pulling his pants up down to an exact science.

Gretchen fought to keep the smile from her face. It was hard to stay mad at the little imp when he was so endearing. Turning her head slightly so he wouldn't see her eyes laughing, she barked,

"Explain yourself, young man."

"Umm, well...I was...doing a three," Caleb stated. He would have thought that would have been obvious. Maybe, Gretchen was out of the loop or something. She *was* rather on the old side.

"A three. I see. So what exactly is a 'three'?"

"Well, Rascal wouldn't listen, so I had to count like Momma

does. You know…one, two, three? 'Course I'm way smarter than the dog and don't never let it get passed two. If he would of just paid 'tention it wouldn't of happened. When I got to three, he didn't leave me no choice. I had to string him up by his toes, or crazy Rascal would think I didn't know what I was doing."

Caleb's matter of fact explanation was delivered with a straight face. Honest to a fault, the child made it plain he truly believed he had no other choice. He even shook his head over the dog's lack of response.

"Let me get this straight. You were trying to string the dog up by his toes, so the dog wouldn't think *you* were crazy?" Gretchen shook her head. Where did the child come up with this stuff? "If you've never gotten to three before, what makes you so sure your Mom would hang you by your toes?"

"'Cause Tyler said that's what happens."

"Tyler?! How many times have I told you not to listen to that little heathen? He does nothing but make up stories and try to get you in trouble. Which is precisely what's going to happen now. You march yourself upstairs this instant and start cleaning that room of yours. When your mother gets home, we'll discuss a more suitable punishment."

Gretchen's harsh words were laced with a swallowed smile. That child was going to be a handful. If he wasn't getting into something, he was sitting around thinking of ways to get into something. She shook her head, as she watched him start up the stairs.

Her attention was turned when she heard a knocking at the front door. She glanced up at the kitchen clock. Hmm…only 4:15. Too early for Kristian to be home. It was probably another one of those stinking vacuum salesman. Every time she turned around, they were begging to vacuum her carpets and sell her a new machine for the low, low price of nine hundred ninety-nine dollars and ninety-nine cents. Like she needed to blow money out the back end or something. Her old vacuum worked just fine.

By the time she got to the door, she had herself worked into a dither. The no-nonsense scowl was firmly in place, and she flung open the door to give them a piece of her mind.

"Pardon me, Madame. I can leave if this is a bad time." A grin played with the corners of his mouth. Orneriness had taken residence in his eyes and made him look younger than his speckled whiskers allowed. His blue uniform bulged around his muscular arms, and the sun glint off the badge on his chest. He pulled his hat off with leathery hands and made as if to head back to his car.

"Austin, now there ain't no call for that! You get on back here before I have to flip you over my knee."

"My, my…somebody's had a change of heart. The way you answered that door, I was expecting you to clobber me with your rolling pin!"

"I didn't know I was going to find you on the other side of this door, or I wouldn't have jerked it open like that. I figured you was a durn salesman. Always coming around here throwing dirt on my clean floors to show me how good their vacuum is."

"Easy now, you're going to get yourself all worked up again," he countered. He liked to watch her get riled up and felt sorry for any salesman that crossed her path.

"What brings you up here this time a day? Kristian ain't gonna be off for another hour or so. You know that."

"You mean, she's not here?" he asked. He shifted his weight and looked puzzled. He'd just come from her office, and they said she'd left early. Austin had gone by in the hopes of surprising her with a pair of tickets to the sold out Rascal Flatts concert. One of the junior officers was planning to go, but his wife had gone into labor on him. He'd reluctantly given them up, cursing his wife for her inconsiderate timing.

"What kind of question is that? You know that woman can't get away from those people until well after five. Always coming in with one more hard luck story to tie her down. Kristian's heart's too big for her britches, if you ask me."

By "those people," she meant the women who came to the abuse shelter looking for assistance. Kristian was the head of social services for domestic violence in the local area. This included some of the spill over from the larger cities. She was renowned for her compassion for the abused and her spunk when it came to prosecuting the abuser. Her quick wit on the stand and knowledge of domestic laws made her a formidable foe in court. Defense attorney's never knew what hit them. They would be so caught up looking at her curves and full lips, they missed the intelligence that lurked in her green eyes. Kristian kept her dark hair just above the shoulders, and it framed her heart shaped face. She could draw the room's attention and still be totally oblivious to the stares. The air of innocence was one of the things that made her so captivating. It was refreshing to be around someone whose beauty was genuine on the inside as well as out.

Austin couldn't help noticing the protective disdain in Gretchen's voice. She had the suspicion that everyone was out to take advantage of her employer. Ever since Kristian had moved to Fort Wayne, she had made it her personal responsibility to look after her. Nearly three years ago, she was hired on as a nanny to Caleb and had grown to be one of the family. As far as Gretchen was concerned, there was always some lowlife who was worming their way into Kristian's kindness, so they could twist it to their benefit. Problem was, try as she might, she couldn't convince Kristian of that. Always the optimist, she naively believed deep down there was some good in everybody. She'd believe any sob story and worked herself into the ground trying to help.

"Well, I was just at her office, and they said she left over an hour ago," Austin replied. "I just assumed she'd taken the afternoon off to play with Caleb."

The lines on Gretchen's forehead frowned, and she pursed her lips in thought. Had Kristian told her she had some errand to run, and she'd let it slip her mind? Surely, not. She was usually pretty good at remembering such things.

"She's not been by here. I could have swore she told me she had a lot to get done on the Walker case, and she wouldn't be home 'til late. That dang Ronnie is really puttin' up a fight. He's been flouting that restraining order and is trying to convince Cindy to drop the abuse charges. Man nearly kills her and thinks they should just kiss and make up. Cretans like that ought to be horse whipped and left to die. Can you believe such a thing?"

Austin chose to ignore the horse whipping comment and honed in on the fact that Kristian hadn't been by the house yet. That wasn't like her to get some unexpected time off and not spend it with her son. She was one of those mothers who made it a point to be her child's best friend. The two were nearly inseparable. In fact, it wasn't unusual to find the two out in the back yard playing cowboys and Indians until well after dusk.

"When she does come in, could you have her call me? I've got a surprise for her and wanted to see if she would be free tonight. I'd stay and wait, but the chief needs me to go check on the widow Sanders. Apparently, she's convinced there's a prowler in the neighborhood and wants us to set up a stake out."

He rolled his eyes, as he put his hat back on. They'd recently arrested a bunch of teens last month for vandalism. Ever since, old Mrs. Sanders was convinced anyone not old enough to shave was a prowler. The chief was getting tired of fielding her incessant phone calls. Her husband had been a prominent member of the Fort Wayne community, and his widow still had the financials to do some damage to the department if things didn't go her way. Chief Brody wanted to tell her to stick a sock in it, but he couldn't afford to make her an enemy. That's why he'd sent Austin to handle her complaint this time. He knew he could count on Austin to hold his tongue and make the old hag feel like she was being listened to.

Chapter 3

Time and hatred made his jaw line haggard and accentuated the wrinkles around his eyes. Sweat dripped off of his hawk like nose and settled in the scar just above his lip. He reached up to brush it away with a dirty hand. The smudge only added to his disheveled appearance. He'd spent the last several hours digging a hole big enough for his prey. It had been easier than expected. Right next to a creek he found an opening to an underground cave. With a little grunt work, he managed to make it wide enough for his purposes. The cave itself was deeper than it was wide. The walls were only four feet apart, but the bottom was at least eight feet down. A small creek fed into it, but the only way out was up.

He wanted everything to be perfect. It had taken him nearly two years to find her, and he wanted to enjoy his revenge. His stint in prison gave him plenty of time to fuel his rage. Cole had found Kristian before she was tainted and had given her his heart. Of course, like those before her, she could never be satisfied with what she had once the ring was on her finger.

It started out subtle at first. Wearing makeup and clothes to exsentuate her assets, then staying out late claiming to be doing research at the library. He'd bought into her studious act at first but soon realized she was taking advantage of his trust. He could see how those men were ogling her. The slut didn't even have the decency to cover herself up when she went out. Like she didn't know wearing shorts with those long, sensuous legs was going to attract attention. They groped her with their eyes, and she always stopped to talk when they shouted something her direction.

Just thinking about it made his heart pound and his fist ache. He'd tried to do the right thing. Like his Daddy always said, if your woman don't mind then you got to knock some sense into her. Literally. Cole attempted to bring her around, but she was already ruint. No matter how hard he tried, she refused to listen. Always called his hand and forced him to punish her. It was for her own good. He didn't want to, but he didn't deserve to have a back stabbing whore for a wife.

His eyes narrowed, as he thought about the way the judge dismissed him in court. He'd already decided Cole was guilty before he even heard his side of the story. One look at Kristian's angelic face and voluptuous chest was all he needed. Dirty bastard, he was probably panting to get in line with the others who wanted a piece of her. No matter though, that judge had done him a favor when he sent him to jail. It gave him a chance to distance himself from her charms, so he could think of a suitable way to discipline her. She would pay for her transgressions.

Leaves crunched under Cole's feet, as he made his way back to a borrowed jeep. He took in a deep breath of the fresh spring air and relished his freedom. The trees rustled slightly in the evening breeze and made shadows cavort across the ground. Last week at this time, he sat in his cell wondering if his contacts were ever going to find her. The wench had taken his son and vanished after the trial. None of the locals knew she was leaving until she didn't turn up for classes the following week. From the looks of it, she'd taken all she could pack in her SUV, drained her formidable bank account, and driven off in the night.

A friend of a friend he'd made in prison gave him the number to a shady "bounty" hunter of sorts. For a small fee, he'd track down anyone, dead or alive. Cole had made it quite plain he wanted Kristian alive for his purposes. He needed to look her in the eye when she breathed her last.

He'd nearly given up hope of ever locating her when he got the letter. Apparently, his contact had a stroke of luck when he was up visiting some relatives in Fort Wayne. His cousin, Ronnie Walker, was moaning about this knockout in social services who was trying to nail his butt to the wall. His bitch wife had gone to her for advise after he'd knocked her around. According to Tony, his wife kept running into his fist with her face. Go figure. Wasn't like he'd killed her or nothin', but this social services woman had gotten Cindy under her thumb while she was recovering in the hospital. The woman had his old lady convinced she deserved better than to be his punching bag. She'd even helped her file for a restraining order and planned to testify at the domestic assault trial. Cindy would have already been back cooking his supper if it weren't for that do-gooder, Kristian.

Needless to say, it wasn't long before the bounty hunter put it all togethor. He followed Kristian around for a while to pick up her habits. It made his mouth water to watch her sashay down the street on the way to her office. Women like her needed a good man around to remind them why they were women. He was tempted to make a move on her himself before he turned her over to Cole. It'd been a while since he'd had a fine woman's legs wrapped around him. Unfortunately, she was serious about some local yocal cop. What a waste. Rather than risk it with lover boy, he just sent a note down to the Alabama State Penitentiary.

Somehow, it didn't surprise Cole to find out that Kristian had another man wrapped around her finger. It made his stomach turn to think about another man putting his hands on his wife. The slut never did know how to honor and obey. What made it worse, she never had a lack of men panting at her door.

Seeing her again nearly unnerved him. He was headed back to the jeep when he heard a steady thump...crunch... thump...crunch in the woods behind him. His heart started racing, and he'd dashed behind the nearest tree. Half of Alabama was out searching for him. He had visions of being cuffed before he had the opportunity to implement his plan. The thumping in his chest made it hard to hold still. Every muscle was stretched tight in readiness for a fight. When she came into view, it took his breath away. Jogging pants clung to her legs, and a snug T-shirt tried to contain ample breasts. Her dark hair was flying loose behind her and accentuated her flushed face. She stared straight ahead and looked lost in thought.

He couldn't take his eyes off her. She was more beautiful than he remembered, and he had the overwhelming need to hold her. The ache started in his arms and spread to his lips. What he wouldn't give to have her pressed against him, with her succulent lips parted in anticipation. It'd been too long since he'd exercised his husbandly rights.

He'd had to shift positions to keep his desire under control. The last thing he needed right now was to let his urges cloud his judgment. A twig snapped when he leaned back, and her head snapped up at the sound. She swiveled her head in his direction, as her dark eyes scanned the trees. They riveted on him. Her gaze penetrated his face and seemed to bore into his brain. Confusion clouded her forehead, as she tried to focus on what she was seeing. When his presence registered, he was close enough to watch the color drain from her face.

Kristian stumbled to a stop, and her jaw dropped open as if to scream. Her muscles didn't want to cooperate with her. The flight response was urging her to go, but disbelief had her paralyzed. Cole couldn't stop the satisfied grin on his face. He'd waited so long for this moment, and it was gratifying to know that he still welded the power. She knew who was in charge even if she was too stubborn to admit it.

In an instant, she turned and bolted. He was right on her heals. A laugh grumbled up from his belly when he saw where she was headed. Cole thought he was going to have to spend days stalking his prey. The holding cell he'd fashioned was going to have a visitor much sooner than anticipated.

She rounded the tree he'd used as a visual marker for the cave. Kristian glanced behind her to see if he was still there, and the ground vanished beneath her. The opening swallowed her, and the last thing he saw was her hair slip below the ground. The muted the scream of terror was cut short with a dull thud.

Cole ran up to the gapping hole and peered down. One leg was at a crazy angle, and her hair was splayed out over a rock. From his vantage, he couldn't discern any movement. Come on and move, damn it, he'd cursed inwardly. He hadn't gone to all this trouble for her to just die on him. Laying down on his stomach, he peered down at her chest. Much to his relief, her ribs were still moving up and down ever so slightly.

Satisfied that she hadn't expired prematurely, Cole grabbed the plywood lid he'd stashed behind an evergreen. He didn't want someone messing up his plans, so he'd made a makeshift cover for the cave. It fit tight over the opening and he threw some leaves over the top for camouflage. Taking a step back, he eyeballed his handiwork. If he didn't know what he was looking for, he'd swear that nothing looked out of place. Perfect. Everything was running well ahead of schedule

Back at the jeep, Cole put his shovel in the back and started the engine. As he put it into gear, he caught a glimpse of his reflection in the mirror. He was still sporting a five o'clock shadow from two days ago. His last visit with the razor had been right before he let himself out of prison. Those guards never new what hit them. A sardonic grin creased his face as he thought about it. Lucky for them, he was feeling nice and made it painless. His eyes narrowed, and he suddenly felt a surge of eagerness. Kristian was in his clutches, and he'd soon have his son back. He'd teach that wench the meaning of "til death do us part."

Chapter 4

Time oozed by like a bug sliding down an unsuspecting windshield. The darkness made it nearly impossible for Kristian to tell how long she had been lying there. Had it been hours or minutes since she'd hit bottom? She inwardly groaned, as she tried to shift her weight. Every muscle ached from the impact, and her bones were weary from the adrenaline rush. From the feel of things, her body was one solid bruise. Easing her arm around, she was able to reach down to her left leg. Gritting her teeth, she forced herself to touch it. When she got to the knee cap, she cursed. Her left leg was twisted sideways just below the knee. No wonder she couldn't move.

Kristian suddenly became aware of the sticky warmth on the back of her head. She raised her arm and exploring fingers let her know that she was definitely going to need stitches. That is, if she ever made it back to civilization.

It seemed like decades, since she'd been staring her nightmare in the face. A shudder ran down her spine and made goose bumps stand at attention on her arms. She couldn't help wondering if her chills were from the cold water seeping through her pants or merely her fear of him. After all these years, Cole could still reduce her to a whimpering bundle of nerves. How many times had she told women the only way they could control you was if you let them? It was easy to spout off about the need for self-confidence and independent thought to other women. "Face your fears, and you'll soon have nothing left to fear," she'd tell them. Yet, here she was with a busted leg at the bottom of some God forsaken hole because she had turned tail and run.

Kristian closed her eyes and let out a sob. Somehow, the black void was more bearable when her eyelids were sealed. At least then it didn't feel as if it was trying to suffocate her. Hugging herself, she tried to block out the image of his face and that guttural laugh. She'd heard him relishing his power as she was trying to run. How had she let him take over her senses again?

When she'd left Alabama, she swore to herself that Cole would never again have the pleasure of seeing her bow down. Testifying at the trial nearly cost her all of her self respect. It was bad enough her husband had stripped her of her pride but then, to have to tell perfect strangers of all the atrocities she had endured. She still cringed just to think about it. The worst part was having his eyes penetrate her as she answered all the questions his lawyer slung at her. He'd gone out of his way to slander her name and make it look like she was somehow to blame for the situation. If she hadn't known the truth, she might have been convinced herself that she deserved everything she got.

In a way, Kristian thought, she had. Looking back, it was hard to believe she allowed herself to be abused. Sure, the counselors tried to tell her she was a victim, and he was the monster. Yet, hadn't she been the one to stay with the monster and bow to his beck and call? Kristian could feel her face

25

growing warm with embarrassment. The shame washed over her and made her temper flare. How could she have been so stupid, so…so naive? She shook her head and bit her lip to keep from screaming.

Her mind wandered back to the first time she met Cole. Back to when she was young and vulnerable. Before life had scarred her and broken her Pollyanna bubble.

Kristian was pouring over her psychology book in the college commons. Her professor was known for giving pop quizzes, and she was trying to brush up on last night's assignment. She'd intentionally set back in a corner to keep from drawing attention to herself. Most of the students were there to socialize and have a good time at Daddy's expense. The girls were consumed with fashion, drinking and attracting a mate. The guys immersed themselves in alcohol and gaining another notch on the bedpost. Anything intellectual was the farthest thing from their minds, and she had a hard time fitting in. Books were the only companions she found that could stimulate her thoughts and let her truly engage her intelligence.

Cole had come bursting through the doors, and his laughter forced Kristian to look up. Peering over the edge of her book, she watched as every illegible female started preening herself. She remembered rolling her eyes and assuming he was just another frat boy. Probably full of himself and softened by lack of industrial labor.

He appeared unaffected by their attentions, and continued talking to the guy next to him. His hat was pulled low on his forehead. It wasn't until he turned around that she noticed the name badge on his shirt. Upon closer examination, she could see the slacks and polo shirt he wore had the Culligan emblem on them. Her eyes had been drawn to his hands. The leathery skin was littered with callouses that proclaimed the work they'd done.

Kristian found herself staring in amazement. From this angle, she got an uninterrupted view of his face. His cheeks were tanned from the sun, and he had laugh crinkles around the edges of his mouth. Not overly handsome, with his angular nose, yet he had a certain charisma that made him pleasant to look at.

Without even noticing, she had unwittingly laid her book aside and was blatantly gawking at him. He must have felt her eyes, because he suddenly stopped talking and looked her full in the face. She felt the heat rise in her cheeks, and she scrambled to bury herself back in her book. With any luck, her chair would be sucked into a swirling vortex, and she would be whisked away to Oz.

Kristian tried to focus on the page in front of her, but her heart was pounding in her chest. She'd never before been so brazen as to stare at a guy. So many times she'd had them ogling her, she'd not allowed her self the same opportunity. Besides, most of the guys she'd seen thus far had merely been spoiled brats, not men.

"I'll talk at ya later, Stan. I got me some pressing business I need to attend to," Cole said as he clapped his friend on the back.

Kristian nearly choked on a gulp when she realized he was headed in her direction. Oh, Lord, now what was she going to do? She couldn't turn tail and run, he'd already gotten too close. Dang it, dang it, dang it, she inwardly groaned. The one time she'd let herself notice someone of the male persuasion and he'd caught her gawking. What an imbecile!

He stopped beside her, and she could tell he was waiting for her to look up. Huh, she wasn't about to give him that pleasure. If he wanted to stroke his ego, he'd have to do it somewhere else.

"Good book?" He inquired with a hint of sarcasm. From the corner of her eye, she could see his hands were clasped behind his back. He rocked back on his heels and peered down his nose as if he actually had an interest in what she was reading.

Kristian nodded her head slightly without raising her eyes. The words on the page blurred as she tried to force her self to read. Maybe if she ignored him he would vanish.

"Really…that's strange. I could have swore you were bored. What, with the way you were staring at me…" Cole's voice trailed off, but the suggestion of laughter lingered. He was obviously enjoying her discomfort.

She'd tried to keep her eyes diverted from him, but she couldn't help flinching at his accusation. The color stained her cheeks, and she gave him a haughty stare. How dare he blatantly confront her like that? If he was any kind of gentleman, he would have just let it ride. But, oh no, he had to come over to rub it in her face. She couldn't trust her voice to be steady, or she would have told him so.

Stiffening her spine, she opted to ignore the question and shifted away from him in her seat. She grabbed her pen and attempted to look busy with her notebook.

"So…what is this 'good' book about?" He leaned over, so he could read over her shoulder. She hadn't really focused on the words until he was breathing down her neck. Right in the center of the page was a newspaper blurb highlighting the causes of sexual deviance. The title "Rape: A Crime of Passion or Power?" leapt out and painted Kristian's face crimson. Great, now he was going to think she was rude and perverted.

"Well, well, well…that explains a lot. Brushing up on wayward sex fiends? Very interesting indeed!" His lips twitched with unvented laughter, and he rasied an eyebrow inquisitively.

The hairs stood up on the back of her neck while Kristian tried to maintain her composure. How dare he provoke her when it was obvious she was already uncomfortable? Typical male, she thought, always gloating when they had the upper hand. She stole a glance at him through lowered lids and could tell by his body language he was enjoying himself immensely.

Why wouldn't he just go away? It wasn't like she asked him to come over and chat it up. Okay, so maybe she'd been staring, but that didn't mean she wanted to carry on a conversation.

Taking her time, Kristian slowly brushed a stray hair from her face and pretended not to see him. Yet, as hard as she tried, she couldn't ignore how his presence made her heart race and her words fail. Always the queen of debate, it was unusual for her tongue to be tied. *Go away*, she prayed silently.

"Come now, seeing as we share…similar interests…surely you could take a few minutes to talk. Personally, I think rape is both." He brushed her shoulder as he reached out to point to the article. Leaning into her ear, he whispered, "It's not power or passion…merely a powerful passion!" He took a step back as he waited for her response.

In spite of herself, Kristian's head snapped up and her eyes blazed. What an insensitive Cretan to crack jokes about something as serious as a man forcing himself on a woman. Glaring at him, she retorted,

"Thank you for that insightful observation. Now, if you'll excuse me,…" She took an exaggerated look at his name badge before she continued. "…Cole, I have better things to do than discuss sexual deviation with someone whose thought process is so asinine."

Kristian stood to gather her books. As she stuffed them into her satchel, Cole side stepped so she could see him in her peripheral vision.

"Well, now, that does pose a problem, doesn't it? Here I thought you were admiring me for my brains, and you were just lusting after my body. Makes me feel rather violated."

His laughter followed her out of the commons making her retreat even more humiliating. Those eyes bore through her back and made her feel like he could see into her thoughts.

After that first rocky encounter, Kristian found herself shadowed by a quick-witted Culligan man. Cole went out of his way to goad her into a sassy response. She began to anticipate his interruptions and actually thought of come backs in advance. One thing led to another and she was soon wed to the "most eligible bachelor" on campus. He made friends everywhere he went, and he knew just how to make her laugh. With him, life wasn't such a serious occasion. Laughter and fun became a welcomed change to her routine.

Of course, that was the pre-wedding band era. Something about that shiny circle reacted like a catalyst in Cole's transformation. He underwent a Dr. Jekyl and Mr. Hyde make over not long after the vows. In public, he was the same easy going comedian. Lovable and charming to a fault, not a single person had a bad thing to say about him. But…at night, when the sun went down and the audience was gone, the demon broke free. Nights out with the boys turned into painful sparring matches for Kristian. The alcohol created dreadful accusations and uncertain fear. Would he be full of loathing and unvented anger? Or would he be too exhausted to follow through?

The torment was subtle, at first. Cole would question her whereabouts and made snide comments about her clothes. Words turned into weapons of manipulation and hands turned into steel reminders.

Something slimy slithered across Kristian's leg and brought her back to the present. She flinched making white pain shoot up her leg. It settled in her eyes causing her insides to start spinning. The dizziness triggered nausea, and she fought to keep her stomach down.

Closing her eyes tight, Kristian silently tried to pray. Thoughts bumped into each other, but the words wouldn't come. Utterly exhausted, she began mouthing the bedtime prayer she'd taught Cole.

"Now I lay me down to sleep. I pray the Lord my soul to keep. If I shall die…" A sob lurched to her throat, making it impossible to finish. The truth in the statement choked her up. Death wasn't quite as quaint when it was breathing down your neck.

Chapter 5

The sun glint off the windshield, forcing Austin to shield his eyes. The angle was horrible this time of evening. Light played tricks with the pavement and made driving nearly impossible.

Glancing at his watch, he was surprised to see it was nearly six. His encounter with the enraged widow Sanders took longer than expected. She nearly talked his ear off about "kids these days." No respect for anybody or anything. Her slight frame shook as she ranted and her wrinkles started to dance. It's a wonder she didn't rattle herself apart, Austin thought.

He'd gone to ask her about a specific complaint she'd called in, and the eighty year old wanted to talk generalities. Those hooligans were eyeballing her the other day, and she knew they'd jump her given the chance. They were always out cruising the streets with loud music blaring. Couldn't hear yourself think with all that racket. If the widow had her way, anyone under eighteen would be forced into manual labor and taught to be seen, not heard.

A smile tickled Austin's lips at the irony. Old jabber jaws herself wanting someone else to be silent. Guess Momma was right, the mouth is always the last thing to go.

Austin pulled into the station parking lot and had to stand on his brakes. Tires squawking, he nearly clipped Lewinsky before he got stopped. New to the force, the kid had more enthusiasm than brains. He dwarfed Austin with his long legs and overdeveloped frame. The bulk wasn't chiseled so much as pudgy around the edges. He reminded Austin of an overgrown toddler with his rounded features and clumsy gait. At least his heart was in the right place. Problem was, his body didn't always follow suit.

When Austin rounded the corner into the lot, Lewinsky was barreling across. Head down, arms pumping, he'd stepped right in front of his car. Austin's protesting brakes made Lewinsky look up. Eyes bulging, he lurched to get out of the way. The front fender missed his knee by inches.

"You all right?" Austin hollered as he opened his door. His heart was still racing from the near miss.

Lewinsky looked dazed as he quickly patted himself down. He stuck up a meaty paw and sputtered,

"Yeah...yeah...I'm okay. I think. Might have to change my drawers, but otherwise I'm good to go." His voice shook slightly, and he nervously adjusted his shirt.

Austin walked over and patted him on the back. Poor kid looked like he'd seen a ghost. The color in his face had drained to where it matched the undershirt that was peeping out of his uniform.

"Where you headed in such a hurry anyway? I didn't see you until you were right there in front of me."

Lewinsky reached up a scratched his head.

"Where was I going?" His voice trailed off in question. He rolled his eyes up like he might find the answer written on his eyebrows. Was he even going somewhere? It was obvious from his facial expression that the hamster had temporarily left the wheel.

Well, he'd been sitting at his desk pushing through yesterday's paperwork. His chair was leaned back in a permanent reclined position, and his legs stretched out under his desk. Chief Brody stormed in slamming things around. The vein in his neck was going, so Lewinsky had tried to lay low. That was easier said than done at his size. His feet were sticking out the opposite side of his desk. All size thirteen of them were dangling in the walkway.

The chief was waiving a sheet of paper over his head ranting about the bad timing of criminals. In his haste, Brody stumbled over the bulky appendages. Fortunately, the trash can broke his fall, spewing fast food wrappers and donut carcasses everywhere.

"What in the hell are you doing, boy?" He yelled as he jumped back to his feet. His eyes blazed adding fuel to his tirade. The stream of profanities that followed would have made an ex-con blush.

By the time the tongue lashing was over, Lewinsky needed a new rear end and a pair of pants to house it in. Once Brody finally calmed down, he set in again about some all points bulletin he'd just received from the bureau. Apparently, a "scum-bum" had busted out of the Alabama penitentiary. Ordinarily, that would be of no concern to their precinct at Fort Wayne. But, this was no ordinary jail break. The low life had left two bodies in his wake. To make matters worse, one of the guards he slaughtered was an under cover agent. The bureau had spent months getting him established in the prison. They had suspected for some time that the warden was involved in a major drug ring. He was a smooth talking s.o.b. who'd been evading charges for years. All they'd needed was a little more evidence, and they could have busted the largest drug smuggling ring in the southern states.

That was blown all to Hades when their main informant was found with his nose rammed into his brain. Now, the FBI had their underwear in a bunch and had jumped into the man hunt. All of the inmates who had any contact with the escapee were grilled. Hours were wasted questioning and requestioning guys whose criminal records made them less than reliable. Apparently, they were in hopes that one of them would know where he was headed or at least what his motive was. The imbecile was up for parole in six months. He was as good as out of there with his record of "good behavior." Something big must be going down for him to risk the death penalty when freedom was within his reach.

The investigator conducting the battering was about to give up hope of getting anyone to squeal when he hit pay dirt. The cell mate finally admitted that he "might" know something. His ailing memory had to be coaxed with the promise of a shortened sentence. When the carrot was dangled, it didn't take long to refresh his ailing mind.

It seems Frankie had over heard the wanted making arrangements to go to Wyoming. He'd been muttering about a "nice piece of ass" that had his name written all over it. The plan was to pay her a visit to remind her of old times. Miraculously, with the help of extra cigarettes and phone privileges, Frankie recalled that the "ass" in question resided around Fort Wayne.

The chief thought it convenient that all of the information came from a convict who was exchanging recollections for personal gain. It didn't help Brody's disposition when he was expected to put his men on full alert based on the flimsy details. According to the bulletin, the FBI would be sending a "man" to head up the investigation. Until he arrived, Brody was to organize his officers to monitor the traffic going in and out of the city. Some would be conducting the road blocks and others were to be searching the city for any sign of the wayward fiend. They were supposed to drop everything and look for someone who "might" be coming their way.

As far as Brody was concerned, the whole fiasco was nothing but a waste of time. The missing lunatic was probably in Florida kicked back on the beach and enjoying the view. That's were he'd be if he'd just busted out of the pokey. Sand, sun, booze and half naked women…what more could a guy want? While he was lapping it up with a beach bimbo, Brody's men were going to be working overtime trying to secure the perimeter.

Not only were the odds against the murdering bastard being in Fort Wayne, the FBI was coming to turn it into a real nightmare. Some bossy agent would come in and rearrange any provisions Brody initiated. Tight assed bunch of paper pushers who thought their crap didn't stink, that's all he had gleaned from his few encounters with them. Always breezing in and snapping orders like he was supposed to say "how high" or something. Brody had a news flash for them, this detective wasn't going to be anybody's squaw. Not if he could help it.

To make matters worse, his wife had been planning one of her hoity-toity shindigs. She'd invited everybody and their dog to some formal dinner tonight. The in-laws were even coming in to grace tonight's stuffy affair. Nothing worse than a whole room full of holier than thou social butterflies. The women always flocked into clicks and looked down their noses at each other. So in so's dress was just completely out of fashion and have you heard the latest gossip about so and so's husband? Pampered old hens, if you asked him. Chrissy was going to skin him alive when she found out he would be unable to attend.

Tripping over Lewinsky may have been the best thing he'd

done all afternoon. He'd send that buffoon to drop the bomb on his beloved. Surely, she wouldn't kill the messenger. Even if she did, it wouldn't be that big a loss. He'd have to make a mental note to avoid answering the phone in his office. The last thing he needed was an hysterical women ripping him a new one. The FBI would be here soon enough to do that.

"Lewinsky, I got a job for you. Do you think you can manage to deliver a message to Chrissy? Let her know that the FBI will have me otherwise occupied, and I will be unable to escort her to tonight's festivities. I'm heart broke, sorry and all that. Play it up, boy. And if you aren't back here in under an hour I'll have you put on permanent file duty. Understand?"

The anger lingering in his stance added punch to his threat. Lewinsky eagerly replied,

"Yes, sir. No problem, sir. I'll get right on it, sir!" He reached down to pick up the mess his unfortunate legs had caused.

"Enough with the sirs, boy. Get your ass out that door and do what I asked. I swear, if Chrissy isn't thoroughly convinced of my sincere regret…"

"I'm on it, sir…err I mean…uhh"

"Just move it!!"

With that, Lewinsky bolted out of the office and into the path of Austin's cruiser. As the details flooded over him, Lewinsky went white again.

"Oh, man. I gotta go, Austin. Brody's going to eat my ass for supper and have my offspring for a midnight snack. I'm supposed to be filling Chrissy in on the details of why Brody can't be at her dinner tonight."

Austin looked at the baffled boy like he'd lost his mind. His ramblings made absolutely no sense.

"Slow down, there. What does talking to Chrissy have to do

with you nearly getting run over? You're not making any sense."

Lewinsky quickly gave him a run down of what had happened in the office. He didn't stick around to fill in the details. Austin watched him squall his tires on the way out of the parking lot and went inside to investigate.

A man hunt here in sleepy Fort Wayne. As much as the detective in him wanted the thrill of the chase, part of him was disappointed. He'd been looking forward to having a romantic evening with Kristian. It wasn't often that he could wow her with concert tickets. Truth be known, they seldom did anything without Caleb. Not that he minded, Caleb was a blessing and rather entertaining. However, every now and again, he needed to have the momma all to himself. Guess he'd have to wait until another time to get her undivided attention.

Chapter 6

The water felt good running down his back, even if it was lukewarm. His clothes lay in a dirty heap right next to the unidentifiable stain on the floor. It had a certain mud quality with a hint of something more sinister. He didn't know who the previous resident had been, but he had a pretty handy setup. The inch of dust covering the limited furniture let Cole know the occupants hadn't been there for quite some time.

Cole lucked upon his current hideout while he was wandering through the woods outside Fort Wayne. He'd been taking his time trying to get a feel for his surroundings. With the law out combing the country for him, he couldn't be to careful. An inner debate between his desire for creature comforts and the fugitive desire to stay out of sight had been waging all day. His first instinct was to find him a motel. One of those shady numbers where no questions were asked and he was allowed to remain in the shadows. The draw back to that was the trail it would leave. Sure, he could use a false name, but the less contact he had with people, the more likely he would be to avoid a one way ticket back to the pen. Fortunately, the cabin offered him solitude and the perfect place to park his jeep.

Tucked back up in the woods, no one would notice him or his borrowed wheels.

As he stepped out of the shower, Cole grinned at his splintered reflection. A broken mirror hung cockeyed on the wall beside him. Its wooden frame kept the pieces from falling and created the illusion that he was a Picasso original. He started to dry off with a worn out excuse for a towel and surveyed his temporary home. It wasn't much, but it was a lot better than what he'd come from.

Standing in the makeshift bathroom, he could see the entire one room shack. The shower stall and rusted sink sat directly across from the "bedroom." A hammock was stretched across the far corner. The ends were tacked into the wall with steel pipes. On the floor below were several blankets and a pillow. They lay haphazardly as if the previous occupant had rolled out of the hammock and just left them lay.

In the center of the room was an orange love seat. Its fuzzy arm rests and cushions were wore slick in the spots that had seen the most traffic. Judging from the sag in the middle, the springs must have been shot. Between the dust and the escaping stuffing, Cole figured he'd leave it to the mice.

Back in the far left corner stood a cockeyed table with three mismatched chairs. They slumped forlornly in front of an old gas cook stove. A layer of grime had settled over the top and added to the decor. Several cabinets were nailed above the stove and along the wall beside it. Wrapped in the thinning towel, Cole went to explore. His stomach had been growling ever since his little "exercise" in the woods.

Much to his delight, the shelves were stocked with canned goods and beef jerky. Scanning the labels he located a can of chunky beef stew and grabbed a package of dried beef. With a little investigation, he found a hand held can opener and a broken down pan. In no time, he was settled in a wobbly chair to enjoy his feast.

As he wolfed down supper, his mind began to wander over his immediate plans. He couldn't believe he already had her contained. He'd been fantasizing about the day when he would put her back in her place. The thrill of the hunt had been what kept him motivated in that hell hole he'd been forced into. Day and night staring at bars with over grown brutes who'd somehow gotten in touch with their gay side. Nothing like a game of hide and seek to avoid being some guy's bitch. Made his skin crawl just to think about it.

His blood boiled, and a nerve below his eye started to twitch. She had done that to him. Kristian, the good for nothing slut, had stole his freedom and his son. For that, she would pay the ultimate price. He'd loved her, given her a home. Hell, he'd even gone the extra mile to knock some sense into her when she started to stray. Somehow, that wasn't good enough for her. She'd stripped him of his pride, and he'd see to it she felt the consequences.

Slurping down the last of his stew, Cole leaned back and let out a hearty belch. It echoed off the walls and added momentum to his planning. The way he had it figured, those know nothing cops were probably still scrambling around looking for a lead to his whereabouts. He was just cocky enough to believe he still had a few days before he needed to worry about that end of it. That would give him plenty of time to locate his son. Since Kristian was already neutralized, nabbing Cole would be a cinch. Poor kid, she'd probably warped him.

Sucking a stray piece of beef from his teeth, Cole reached for his transistor radio. Static filled the room when he flipped the power switch. He turned the knob searching for a good station. Anything to fill the void and help him relax. His nerves were keyed up in anticipation. Every extremity twitched with the excitement of being so close. It was all he could do to keep from going back to his self fashioned prison to check on his ward. The thought of listening to her whimper and cower under his command sent a jolt of testosterone through his body.

Cole rolled the knob back and forth trying to get reception. His only answer so far had been some intermittent buzzing and pops. Finally, the dial picked up a local radio station. The sounds of the Eagles came drifting into the emptiness. "Welcome to the hotel California…" He started singing along and let the rhythm tap his foot. A sardonic smile stole over his face when he got to the part "such a lovely place…such a lovely face." Kristian's dark eyes and alluring face came to mind. Lovely for now, but he'd see to that a lot sooner than father time.

Chapter 7

Gretchen stood in the kitchen tapping her chin with a spoon. Supper had been done for nearly an hour and Kristian still hadn't turned up. She was never late for dinner. Well, never late, that is, unless she'd already called to let Gretchen know where she was.

Gretchen unconsciously started humming "where oh where are you tonight…" She was having flash backs to her Hee-Haw days. Her late husband would sit down every Monday night and watch the latest country talents. George used to laugh at the goof balls in the cornfield and always liked to "theewwp, you was gone." He'd stick his tongue through his lips and blow. The slobbers would fly, and she'd have to resist the urge to smack him upside his knobby head. Those were the days, she thought with a sigh

Before she could get too lost in thought, Caleb came peeping around the corner. His face was twisted into his most sorrowful look, and he had his hands clasped behind his back. From the expression in his eyes, he'd obviously been contemplating very hard. The last time Gretchen checked on his room cleaning, she'd told him not to come down until he'd thought about what he had done. The poor dog was probably still recovering from this latest escapade.

"Well, don't just stand there lurking in the door way," Gretchen warned. "Best get on in here and tell me what's on your mind."

The boy trudged into the kitchen and stopped just shy of the bar. He took one foot and started tracing the design on the floor. Back and forth around the octagon trimming as he bit on his lower lip. With an intake of breath, he opened his mouth to speak. Before any intelligible words came out, his lips clamped tight. Caleb looked at his feet and shook his head from side to side.

"Now, boy, I haven't got time for your shenanigans. Your momma's runnin' late, my spaghetti's getting cold, and I still gotta get a hold of Austin. It'd be best for everyone involved if you'd just spill it."

Caleb scrunched up his nose and looked at her through lidded eyes.

"But…'yer' gonna get mad at me."

Looking at his contrite face and his ever present dimple, Gretchen had a hard time not smiling.

"No, I won't. As long as you're honest, I won't get upset."

"Yuh-huh, you will. 'Cause, I thunked and thunked about it like you said and tried real hard to be sorry and learn from it like I'm 'posed to…but…well, I think even God might be mad at me now. I don't want you to not like me no more or have to got to the bad place…but I learned something I don't think I was 'posed to."

It was obvious from the anxiety on his face, the poor child honestly thought he'd eaten the forbidden fruit. He was being kicked out of Eden, and his heart was broken. Gretchen bit her upper lip to keep from grinning. The last thing Caleb needed was to have his situation laughed at.

Swallowing a giggle Gretchen solemnly asked, "What did you learn? I promise not to get upset. Whatever it is, we can work it out together."

She could see him mulling it over. The idea of getting it off his chest was very appealing. Maybe, just maybe, Gretchen would stick up for him. That is, if she didn't paddle him first.

"My Sunday school teacher is a liar!" Caleb blurted out. He unconsciously took a step back to get out of arms reach. Visions of Gretchen back handing him flashed before his eyes. She could pack a wallop when she wanted to.

Of all the things he could have said, Gretchen was completely blind-sided by his revelation. How in the world could his little mind connect his Sunday school teacher to his crime? Last time she checked Mrs. Vanhaven was as honest as the day was long. Besides, she was also the biggest dog lover in town and would have been appalled at Caleb's attempt to string up Rascal. The child just wasn't making any sense.

"What in God's name are you talking about? Mrs. Vanhaven probably never told a lie her whole life, and she sure ain't had nothing to do with your time out." Gretchen's no nonsense tone made Caleb stiffen his spine. No matter how Gretchen might react, he had to stand behind his discovery. He'd spent all afternoon pondering it and now wasn't the time to turn tail.

Clearing his throat for courage, Caleb raised his head. The determination had settled in his eyes and forced him to continue. Mrs. Vanhaven had been fooling people long enough.

"Yes, huh, she is to a liar. Last Sunday, she told us that the truth shall set you free. But that ain't so, 'cause I tell'd you the truth about doing a three and it got me put in time-out. I don't think that's very funny."

Flabbergasted, Gretchen had to struggle to keep from going

slack jawed. At four, this child was already thinking circles around the average male. The sad part was, she could see his four year old perspective. An adult told him freedom comes with the truth, then she puts him in solitary confinement for his trouble.

Gretchen shifted her weight on her feet and tried to buy time by scratching her head. She didn't want to blow it and make Caleb think his logic was right. Yet, somehow the words wouldn't come.

"Honey, I don't think…well…Mrs. Vanhaven didn't mean freedom like you're thinking about. It's more like a freedom from guilt than actually being, well…free." The hesitation was evident in Gretchen's voice, and she could see Caleb scrunching up his eyebrows. A question was brewing behind those inquisitive eyes.

"But, that don't make no sense," Caleb began. "I didn't feel guilt 'bout nothin' until after I told the truth, and you told me I had to."

Kid had a point. Lordy, how was she supposed to keep up with such an advanced thinker? He was always analyzing things to death and making everything so complicated. Why couldn't he just push trucks and make motor noises like the other four year olds?

Gretchen absently stirred her cold spaghetti sauce to buy some time. She glanced towards the door, hoping Kristian would walk in so she could field Mr. Twenty Questions. Unfortunately, she didn't materialize.

"Caleb, you're a big boy now, and someone shouldn't have to tell you when to feel guilty. You know you're not supposed to be aggravating poor ole Rascal. Eventually, your conscience would have toed you in the gut, and you would have felt bad for not listening to your momma. Since you've done told the truth, you won't have to worry over your momma's disappointment. Yawl will get everything out in the open, and life can get back to normal."

Caleb stood still and thought for a minute, "But, Mrs. Vanhaven…" He started.

"No buts!" Gretchen interrupted. The last thing she needed was another inquisition. Her nerves were shot, and she didn't have the patience to deal with it.

"Now, you skadaddle into the bathroom and wash those filthy hands. I'll dish you up some supper as soon as you're cleaned up!"

Squelched, Caleb shrugged and skipped back out the door he came in. Just as he rounded the door jam, he stuck his face back in the kitchen. With an impish grin he announced,

"I love you, Gretchen!" He then bolted down the hall, and she heard the bathroom door slam.

"Ornery little turd," Gretchen muttered under her breath. She shook her head and walked over to the small television set on the cabinet. It was getting time for the local news, and she wanted to keep up on the latest happenings. The screen flickered on, and Dedra Jones sultry voice invaded the kitchen.

"In other news, the national man hunt continues for the escaped convict responsible for the deaths of a prison guard and an undercover FBI agent. Thirty-four year old Cole Williams broke out of the Alabama State Penitentiary late last Wednesday evening. Sources say the FBI has reason to believe Williams may be heading towards the Fort Wayne area. He is considered armed and extremely dangerous. If you have any information that could lead to his apprehension, please call your local law enforcement."

The mug shot of a glaring male in a prison orange jump suit filled the screen. His sullen eyes and hawk like nose made

Gretchen's skin crawl. To think, that lowlife was heading their direction. Makes a body wonder what he was after in such a sleepy little town. Wasn't like they had anything flashy to offer. The more Gretchen stared, the more she got the sensation that there was something familiar about those eyes. And the name. Now, where had she heard of Williams before? Wasn't that one of George's distant relatives? Or maybe it was someone in her bridge clubs nephew? Oh well, it would come to her, eventually. Maybe Kristian would recognize the name when she came home.

Gretchen glanced uneasily at the clock. She'd feel a lot better when she'd heard something out of Kristian. Especially with that criminal possibly prowling around.

Chapter 8

By the time Austin got into the office, the whole place was in pandemonium. He could hear Brody's gruff voice barking orders. Officers were scrambling over top of each other to comply. From the sound of it, they were being divided into surveillance groups to try to cover every inch of the city. Younger, more inexperienced officers were being paired up with the more seasoned street cops.

In the midst of the chaos, Austin spotted Terrance leaning against the wall by the water cooler. He had his legs crossed lazily and was watching the scene with a smirk on his leathery face. He'd come to the force from the LAPD, and it was obvious that he found the chief rather amusing. He was used to the blood, guts and ass flying everywhere in the big city, so the small town hype over a man hunt seemed a bit ridiculous. Most of his field experience was in homicide, so ferreting out murderers was almost second nature to him.

Terrance looked up and caught Austin's eye. He raised an eyebrow, then thumbed his nose towards the chief. Austin threaded his way through the desks, trying to avoid being run over in the process. The office was beginning to look like the opening scene from Kindergarten Cop. All Brody needed was a whistle and a pair of sweat pants.

"So, how goes it with the old hag?" Terrance inquired as Austin eased up beside him. The hag in question was the widow Sanders. Poor Terrance was initially welcomed to the community by having the woman whack him over the head with her cane. She'd been hollering citizens arrest over some juveniles crossing her path. During her little tantrum, her feet had slipped, and she lost her balance. Terrance tried to assist her in his off duty attire, ragged blue jeans and a worn leather jacket. She'd mistaken him for one of the thugs and cracked him a good one.

Austin grinned mischievously, "Not nearly as exciting as it has been here. Of course, the dear, sweet lady did inquire about you."

"Oh, really? The old biddy wanna know if she could come brow beat me again? Probably wants to stay in shape in case some hoodlum tries to molest her."

"Naw. She just wanted to know if that 'scalawag lowlife' was still sporting a badge. I got the full fledge what's the world coming to lecture. Apparently, your street clothes made quite an impression."

Terrance rolled his eyes. He should've let her fall and break her face. Wasn't like anyone would really notice the difference with all those wrinkles she was packing around. Would've saved him a scar and a splitting headache.

"That woman needs to be put away in one of those loony bins where they keep the old and decrepit. Maybe, we could all pitch in and buy some tape for her mouth. That way the staff wouldn't have to listen to her rant and rave."

Austin shook his head and laughed. He had to admit, the widow was rather annoying even if she was harmless.

"Speaking of ranting and raving, what's up with Brody? He had Lewinsky so shook up he ran out in front of me. I almost had an over-grown hood ornament."

Before Terrance could respond, Austin heard his name bellowed over the pandemonium.

"Austin, it's about time you got back!" Brody had singled him out of the crowd. His face was red and glistening with drops of frustration. He began waving his ample arms, motioning Austin to join him on the other end of the room. As if to hurry him along, Brody stamped his foot and pointed to the floor in front of him.

Nothing like being treated like a wayward child. Austin swallowed a smart retort and made his way to the spot indicated.

"Might as well bring Terrance, too. You guys are gonna get to know each other *real* well." Brody barked. He turned on his heel and headed into his office. Their compliance was expected, and he never gave either time to respond.

As they walked, Terrance muttered,

"Way to go Austin, you got us both sent to the principal's office. You don't think he'll call my mommy, do ya?"

Austin choked on a surge of laughter. The muscles in the corner of his mouth were fighting the urge to rise into a smile. He had to duck his head when they walked into the chief's office to keep him from seeing his amusement.

Brody was standing behind his desk with his hands clasped behind him. He was looking out of his tiny window at the brick backside of Tubby's Bar and Grill. His office used to over look a vacant lot full of wildflowers. The pub had come in several years ago and taken away any semblance of a view. Of course, whenever he needed to think, Brody always found himself gazing out the window as if those faded bricks were going to guide him in his decision. Turning slowly, he caught a glimpse of the youthful amusement in Austin's eyes. The man was probably thirty years his junior and had a mind like a steel trap. Everytime he watched him in action, he was reminded of all that he'd once been. Huh, Brody was getting too old for this nonsense. He'd been flirting with that notion for the last several months, but this malarkey with the FBI was just ramming it home.

Wiping a wrinkled hand over his face, Brody motioned for Terrance and Austin to sit down. His office furniture consisted of two mismatched leather chairs. They were leftovers from the chief's glory days. He'd hit his prime in the early eighties and was reluctant to let go. Austin got the privilege of sitting in the one that had a crooked leg and a pin hole in the seat cover. When he sat down, air whooshed out and it wobbled precariously to the left.

Terrance wrinkled his nose and waved his hand slightly as if brushing away noxious air. He'd intentionally let Austin have the flagellating furniture. His amusement was quickly reigned in when he saw the seriousness on Brody's face. The man had aged ten years in the last few minutes. His shoulders were slumped with an unnamed burden, and his eyes were riddled with exhaustion. The blustering anger so prominent before the others had been replaced with uncertainty.

Brody walked around and sat on the corner of his desk. Slowly, her ran his hand over his face and prepared to address his two best officers. Terrance had the man hunting skills and Austin was equipped with the people skills to handle any situation. He just hoped they handled it fast enough that the bureau would stay off his ass when they arrived. His last experience with the big dogs had left a sour taste in his mouth. They'd tromped him into the grounds with their filthy regulations and then had the gall to take all the credit when his squad had nabbed the kidnapper. Thanks to his group, they had saved a seven year old boy from the knife and sent a serial pedophile to prison. Of course, that was several life times ago. Back when he was a young, inexperienced cop out to save the world. Time had since taught him that cynicism was the only protection he had against the harsh realities of police work.

Brody shifted his weight. He took the time to look Terrance and Austin in the eye, one at a time. Clearing his throat, he began,

"Well, boys, I guess you know we've been drawn into one hell of a mess. Two guards were murdered and the FBI is in an uproar." Brody stopped when he saw the question mark on Austin's face. He'd just assumed everyone was up to speed on the situation. He'd forgotten that Austin was out baby sitting the neighborhood bag lady when the news came in.

"Somehow an unarmed prisoner managed to take down two guards on his way out of the Alabama State Pen. They were both armed with prison issue weapons, mace and billy clubs, but the escapee got them both with his bare hands. I'll spare you the gory details. The gut clincher is one of the fallen was actually an undercover FBI agent. He'd been on the verge of unveiling one of the biggest drug smuggling operations in the Southern states."

Brody proceeded to fill them in on all the details, including how their sleepy department had been dragged into the fiasco. His eyes snapped, and his jaw shook when he told of how the FBI obtained the tip leading them to Fort Wayne. Nothing like coercing a criminal to gain information. Can't beat the integrity of a man who'd rape his cousin and then squeal on his buddy when promised a lighter sentence.

By the time Brody'd finished his recital of background

information, Brody was back in spit fire mode. The vein in the side of his head began to pulsate in time with his rising voice. His blood pressure was rising from the inside out, and it was helping to fuel his tirade.

"I'm counting on you boys to make this department look good. You're the best we have on the force, so I'm putting you in charge of the internal searching of the town for this lunatic who "might" be here. When those candy-assed pencil pushers waltz in, I want it to be obvious that every rock has been turned over and all the t's have been crossed. I don't want to give them any excuse to hang around this town any longer than necessary. Last thing we need is an all out panic in town. Widow Sanders doesn't need any more reasons to call and harass me."

Terrance gave Austin an all knowing grin. The old hag was getting on everyone's nerves. Austin returned his smile half heartedly. His mind was on the more immediate task at hand. He was being asked to search for a felon that Brody didn't honestly believe existed. Well, at least not in this town. Yet, deep down, he had this nagging feeling there had to be more to it than this. A sense of foreboding was taking up residence in his chest and making his arms tingle with anticipation. It was more of a dread of things to come than an exuberant yearning for what might happen. He knew it was unfounded, but he couldn't keep his stomach from sinking.

Terrance leaned back in his chair and squinted his eyes. The detective inside of him was starting to stir. He'd transferred from the big city to get away from the killers that seemed to breed there. Something about the close quarters and polluted air brought out the worst in people. For years, he was on clean up crew. Trudging out to blood soaked crime scenes in the hopes of finding a clue. Anything that would lead them back to the sadistic bastard responsible before he decided to kill again.

It was usually a matter of time before they tripped up and left there print somewhere. A tangible piece of themselves the force used to snag the sicko. Unfortunately, the capture, as exhilarating as it was, never obliterated the pain for those left behind. The shattered look of loved ones and the heart sinking guilt associated with being the bearer of bad news had taken its toll. It ate away at Terrance's insides until he'd finally had to divorce the situation. When he was at the top of his tracking game, he'd stepped down from the department and vanished into the "middle of nowhere" as his coworkers so aptly called it. He'd thought his desire to ferret out the low lifes had died. Yet, here he was feeling that same rush of adrenaline that always came when a killer needed to be found.

Brody leaned across his desk and picked up a mugshot. He handed the photo to Terrance and said,

"This is who we are supposedly looking for." From where Austin sat he could just make out the vague outline of a man holding up his prison number's.

Terrance gave it the once over and the nerves in his jaw started to tingle. The man was staring into the camera, face full of defiance. His jaw was firmly set under his hawk like nose. At first glance, he reminded Terrance of a doberman pincher waiting to snatch a bite of anyone who passed too close.

Austin leaned over so he could get a closer look, and he was immediately struck by the man's eyes. Something was familiar about the shape of his cheek bones and the way his eyes seemed to radiate a quiet intelligence. He was certain he'd never seen him before, and yet…he couldn't shake the notion that he should know him.

His heart started to pound, and Austin was beginning to think maybe the FBI had a little more insight to the man's location than Brody thought. It made no sense, but his gut was telling him that the guy was close.

"So, what did you say this guy's name was?" Austin asked. His voice betrayed the tension that was building behind his eyes.

"Actually, I didn't say. I believe the name was Williams. Cole Williams. According to the ole FBI 'source,' he's coming to our neck of the woods to find a nice piece of ass with his name on it." Brody chuckled to himself. "Can you believe that nonsense? Why would he travel this far for some broad when he could find plenty of action along the coast? Beautiful women, with assets hanging out all over."

Brody's sarcasm was lost on Austin's backside. In his haste to leave the room, he'd knocked over the chair and the thud echoed in the tiny office. Terrance couldn't be sure, but it sounded like he'd gasped, "oh my God, Kristian," as he bolted out the door.

Chapter 9

Nothing like darkness to drive out sanity and beckon in the demons from the past. Kristian's thoughts shivered against each other in the cold, as she fought to remain conscious. Everytime she started drifting off, memories threatened to march in. Hooded monsters danced around the outskirts of her mind begging for the opportunity to invade her sanity. Her resolve was fading, and Kristian's head kept slipping down towards her chest.

One by one they marched in, full of purpose and ready to snatch her back into the nightmare. It was one she'd finally rid herself of when she poured it out to Austin. He'd coaxed it out of her with his strong arms and soothing words.

Kristian had fallen asleep while they were watching a movie. One of those cowboy jobbies where the good guy always wins. Her head secure in his lap, she could feel Austin stroking her hair absently as Clint Eastwood shot up the screen. She'd seen the movie several times, and the repetitive touch of Austin's had lulled her into oblivion. A place she never went when there were others around to witness her fears.

Looming behind her lids was the fiend. He visited her

several nights a week to remind her of his power. He was the one who'd stripped her of her innocence and forced her to relive the horror of that final night. The night when all hell broke loose and nearly stole her soul.

She'd snapped awake at the sounds of her own screams. Legs thrashing, Kristian had both arms over her face, and she was fighting to catch her breath. Bewildered, Austin called her name and tried to hold her close. Whispering steadily, he kept saying,

"Kristian, hey honey, it's okay. I'm here. It was just a dream."

To his dismay, his voice only served as catalyst for her writhing. The more he attempted to comfort, the harder she fought to get away from him. He'd known the bastard she'd been married to had been abusive but, good Lord! The torment she was in wrenched his heart. Nothing he was doing seemed to help.

It took several minutes for Kristian to fully wake up. Her heart was pounding in her ears, and her body was clammy with sweat. When she'd realized where she was, she'd gone completely limp against Austin. He scooped her up, so she was sitting in his lap. She nestled into his chest and buried her face in his neck.

The tears were silent at first. They trickled down his neck and settled in his collar. The only sound was the forgotten Western. Six shooters clamored in the background echoing off the living room walls. Before long, the flood gates were opened, and the sobs racked her body. Austin felt them slamming through her, as she shook against him. Still, she didn't make a sound other than to gasp for air. She'd learned long ago to cry silently. Noise only fueled the rage and hardened the fists.

Sensing her need for quiet, Austin held her close until the shaking subsided. Leaning his cheek against her hair, he gently brushed a tear from her face with his thumb. Kristian pulled his palm against her lips and murmured, "Thank you."

Her exhaled warmth against his skin was the opening he'd been waiting for. He'd been silently battling whether or not to push Kristian for an explanation. She'd always been vague about her past other than to let him know it was an abusive relationship. No graphic details, just a flat statement of fact and a pleading in her eyes not to ask any questions.

Shifting his weight slightly, Austin asked,

"Do you want to talk about it?"

His voice was throaty with unexpected emotion. Anger at what that monster must have done to Kristian and the fear that she might shut him out, made the question that much harder to ask. She had built up layers of defense to hide her vulnerability. It had taken him nearly a year to break into that inner sanctum. She was just starting to trust him and open up her heart to his love. Austin sensed she'd been gradually relaxing in their relationship. Hell, tonight was all the proof he needed of that. This was the first time she had actually fallen asleep in his presence. Not that he could blame her. After that wretched display, he was surprised she ever slept at all.

Kristian stiffened in his arms, but didn't pull away. His strong chest and the steady bumping of his heart against hers were the only things keeping her sane. This was the first time she'd ever been able to break out of the nightmare within a few minutes. Generally, she teetered in that purgatory where she couldn't fully awaken. Reality and memory were so intertwined Kristian had to wrestle herself back into consciousness. She wasn't ready to talk about it, but she wasn't ready to push Austin out. Not yet, anyway.

Taking her silence as a no, Austin said a silent prayer for courage and decided to plunge ahead. Pushing her forward with his shoulder, he tipped Kristian's head back where he could look into her eyes. Putting his hand on her cheek so he could cradle her face, he whispered,

"How can I help you, if you won't trust me?" Leaning forward he gently kissed her lips. "I love you. Can't you see that?"

The intensity in his eyes and the undemanding pressure of his lips sent a shiver down Kristian's spine. She'd never felt such sincerity or had such a longing to confide in someone. Always hesitant to trust another, she'd learned to rely solely on herself. The demons of the past were hers to fight, and she didn't need to burden Austin with the details. Yet, the warmth of his embrace and his penetrating eyes told her that, somehow, he wouldn't find it a burden. As much as she hated to admit it, she was beginning to need Austin's companionship on a deeper level. Love was something she swore she would never stumble into again after it had destroyed her last time.

Swallowing her misgivings, Kristian decided it was about time to let go of the nightmare. She'd taken so long to convince herself to speak, Austin assumed he'd lost her again. Kristian lowered her head so she was leaning against his chest. She may have been ready to spill her guts, but she wasn't ready to see the horror on his face when she did.

The long silence was broken when Kristian finally stammered,

"It was my fault."

Austin wasn't sure he'd heard her correctly. Before he could question her, she continued,

"I'd been up most of the night with Caleb. He'd been running fever for several days teething, and nothing I could do would satisfy him. Between the wails and the lack of sleep, my nerves were pretty shot."

Kristian could still remember the utter exhaustion she felt walking the floor and humming. Not only were the cries nerve racking, but she knew at any given moment Cole could wake up. Ripping the monster from a dead sleep seemed to be worse than dealing with him as a belligerent drunk.

Since Caleb's birth, it had been her sole responsibility to care for him. Feedings and changing diapers were a must, but above all else she was to keep him silent. Cole couldn't handle the noise and would blame her for any disruption in his life. After all, that squalling mess was her hobby, not his. The inconsolable cries of a newborn were to be squelched, or she would have hell to pay for it.

Usually, she could go into the living room and bounce her son back to sleep. The trick was to stay standing and bobble up and down. This, of course, had to be done to the rhythmic humming of "On the Wings of a Dove." Caleb would drift off to sleep nestled against her shoulder. If she made sure he was good and asleep, she could ever so carefully lay him back in his crib. On that particular night, he was extremely uncooperative. Kristian would have him breathing deep in that 'dead to the world' slumber, but as soon as she stopped bouncing, the screams would commence. Sheer will power had kept her moving until sun up the night before. Cole had already warned her that if she didn't shut that "bastard" up, he'd do it himself. Permanently.

Looking back, she still wasn't quite sure how she managed to do it. In the midst of the bouncing and humming, Kristian had fallen asleep on her feet. Dead to the world, she was oblivious to the pandemonium around her. When she'd snapped out of her trance, Cole was inches from her face screaming vulgarities.

Dazed, Kristian couldn't focus on his words. Her lack of response only served as a catalyst for Cole's rage. Before she could react, he'd snatched Caleb from her arms. Holding him at arms length, he started shaking him violently.

"You worthless piece of shit!! I told you to SHUT-UP!" The maniacal glint in Cole's eyes finally forced Kristian to respond.

"Cole, don't! You'll hurt him. Please, hand him back." The terror in her voice made him laugh sadistically. The sound echoed of the walls above the baby's shallow screams.

"Punch a pillow, hit a wall but never shake a baby!" Cole mocked. His voice had gone up several octaves as he chanted over and over. Each time he said it, the shaking grew harder and more out of control. Caleb's tiny head was bobbling on his shoulders like a tormented rag doll in the mouth of a dog.

Adrenaline kicked in spurring Kristian into motion. Ordinarily, she tried to blend into the scenery during one of Cole's tirades. But, the man had gone too far this time. He could lash at her all he wanted, but he best not mess with her son.

"I believe I told you to stop. Put Caleb down this instant!" The calm forcefulness in her voice surprised even Kristian. It was so out of the ordinary it made Cole pause in his shaking.

He took his eyes off his prey and locked in on Kristian. Her insubordination called for serious rebuke. How dare she take that authoritative tone with him? A sardonic smile crept over his face. Raising Caleb up over his head, he said,

"You want him down, I'll put him down!" With that, he launched the squalling baby across the room. Kristian's heart stopped, as she watched him sailing slow motion away from her. Fortunately, the couch broke his fall. Caleb thudded eerily against the cushions, and the wailing was broken by a gasp for breath. Then, to Kristian's horror, all sounds and movement ceased. She strained to see the subtle up and down motion of Caleb's chest in the shadows. Nothing.

Kristian lunged towards the couch, but Cole was too fast. He stepped in front of her and slapped her across the face with his open palm The stinging brought tears to her eyes and made her head snap sideways. A sharp pain shot down her neck as it popped from the force. Undeterred, she tried to side step around Cole. There had to be a way she could get to Caleb. Her only thought was to hold him close and will him back to life.

Cole managed to grab a handful of Kristian's waist length hair. Wadding it around his hand, he jerked her back towards him.

"Oh, no you don't!" He bellowed. With a string of profanities, he forced Kristian to her knees. Keeping one hand in her hair as an anchor, he used the other to punch her in the jaw.

The sickening thud was soon followed by another and another. He was so enraged that he no longer took aim. Her upper body was showered with blows, and she was soon tasting blood. Kristian began praying silently for the strength to overcome. With God's help, this would be the last time the scum bag ever laid a hand on her. She needed an opening, a distraction, anything to break his concentration. Suddenly, she had an idea.

Going completely limp, she quit struggling to get away. Keeping her eyes closed, she allowed herself to fall to the floor as if she had passed out. Her head snapped as her full weight was held up by the hair in Austin's hand. She bit her lower lip to keep from crying out. Kristian held her breath as Cole relaxed his death grip and shift his weight to get a better look. Disgusted, he shook his head. His 'beloved' never could take a punch.

Just as he leaned over, Kristian jumped up cracking her head full force into his crotch. When Cole doubled over, Kristian blew past him and grabbed Caleb's limp body. She bolted out the front door and towards the car. Her feet pounded the driveway in time with her internal mantra, get away...get away.

Inside the car, she gently lay Caleb in the passenger's seat and scrambled to get the car started. In her haste, she was having trouble getting the key in the ignition. She silently cursed herself for her clumsiness. Why now, dear Lord? Why?

The key clicked into place, and the car roared into life. She was slamming it into reverse when she saw him. Silhouetted in the tail lights, he stood blocking her path. She could just make out the outline of his deer rifle as she jammed it into gear.

Cole's eyes glowed red, and he leered through the back glass. His demeanor was triumphant. He stood between her and the highway, not to mention the fact that he had the slut in his sights. She'd die before she got passed him. Her and the little squall titty she called a son.

Kristian took a deep breath and whispered, "Thy will be done." Gripping the wheel, she stomped the gas. The tires chirped against the concrete, and she lurched backwards towards the demon.

Cole didn't have time to get a shot off as he leapt out of the way. The car teetered on its frame when she jerked it into drive. Her foot never hit the brake on the way through neutral.

Over the hum of the engine, Kristian heard the explosion. Before the sound registered, the glass in the rear passenger window imploded. Chips of glass spewed through the car, and the cold wind whooshed past Kristian's neck. Struggling to keep the tears in check, she concentrated on driving. If she could make it down the deserted highway to the junction, she could get help at the gas station. Ed was a pretty good friend of hers. He'd know what to do.

Kristian's heart sank when headlights blazed into view

behind her. Cole's battered pickup was lumbering up fast. The lights were flickering off her mirror making it hard to concentrate on the road in front of her. *Heaven help me keep it between the lines*, she begged.

Out of nowhere, her rear end began to fish tale out of control. One of Cole's stray bullets sank into her rear tire. Kristian fought the wheel as it jerked her towards the road ditch. She over corrected and swerved off the opposite side of the highway. Her left side slammed into the door, and she felt Caleb plop against her thigh. Looking down, she was relieved to see his eyes wide in terror. His tiny mouth was puckered up in an unspoken wail. The rushing wind and squalling tires drowned out his cries.

Kristian's relief was short lived. When she looked up, a tree loomed in the windshield. It was too late to turn, so she pulled Caleb up against her chest. Using her body as a shield, she doubled over and braced herself for the impact. Metal crunched, glass shattered and the tree groaned at the unexpected attack.

Kristian's shoulder slammed into the steering wheel, and she could feel her collar bone cracking. White hot pain shot down her neck making her head swim. After the sudden stop, the car pitched backwards. The seat felt like concrete as her body was forced into it. Seconds passed like hours until the car finally rocked to a stand still.

Vision blurred, she was having a hard time remembering where she was. Every muscle in her body ached, and the sticky smell of fresh blood was making her nauseous.

Before Kristian could orient herself, Cole was jerking on the door handle. His pulling shook the car but did nothing to move the door. The folded metal had the hinges pinned beneath the front fender. Rage made him jerk harder but to no avail. When that didn't work, he ran back to his truck. He always kept a crow bar behind the back seat.

Kristian's heart thumped in her chest, as she waited silently for his return. Using all her strength, she pushed herself up so she could take a look at Caleb. His eyes were closed, but she could feel his shallow breathing against her chest. Out of the corner of her eye, she spotted her coat laying in the floor board. She'd worn it that morning but forgot to take it in. Gently, Kristian lay Caleb in the folds of the coat and pulled it around him for warmth. Maybe, if she kept Cole distracted, he'd forget about their son. Heaven knew he never remembered him on a normal day.

In a matter of minutes, Cole was standing outside her door. Gripping the iron like a ball bat, he swung at her window. The glass cracked and started to spider web from the center. He drew back again and this time the glass showered in. It rained on Kristian's back, and she could feel it falling down the inside of her shirt. The shards scraped as they settled in the waistband of her pajamas.

Reaching through the window, Cole gripped the back of Kristian's neck. His fingers dug into her sore muscles and made her cry out. Bracing himself against the side of the car, he pulled her out and let her fall to the ground. Too exhausted to fight back, she curled up in a ball. Knees up to her chest, Kristian clasped her hands together in prayer.

Silently moving her lips, she asked God to fill her with his loving strength. Kristian prayed for intervention. Growing up, she'd always been told God would never give you more than you could handle. She just wished he didn't have such a high opinion of her.

Cole nudged her with his boot. When she didn't lookup, he rared back with his crow bar. The blow hit her across the back of the thighs. The whimper that escaped her lips made him thirst for more. This wench would learn to submit or suffer the consequences.

Cole was so wrapped up in his tirade, he didn't see the extra set of headlights pull in behind him. He raised his arms up again, and the crow bar was snatched out of his hands. Whirling around, he saw the old guy from the gas station. In the dark, his six foot, two hundred fifty pound frame looked deadly. The hatred in his eyes was unmistakable. He'd taken a liking to Kristian. She and her son frequented his station, and she always had a kind word to say. Ed wasn't about to stand around while this bastard abused her.

One handed, he grabbed Cole by the throat and slammed him against the car. Slowly, Ed squeezed until he could hear Cole wheezing for air. The boy needed to die. Only the sounds of sirens in the distance kept him from crushing his esophagus.

It was several days later before Kristian found out how Ed came to be her savior. She was recovering in the hospital, and he came to visit. Apparently, he had heard the squalling tires as he was locking up the station for the night. When the sound of the impact followed, he'd gone in to call 911. From the sounds of it, someone was going to be badly hurt. Little did he know he was going to discover a monster when he headed out to investigate.

When Kristian had finished reciting her tale, Austin was too stunned to speak. No wonder she was having problems sleeping. Tightening his grip on her, he whispered,

"The nightmare is over, I'm here to keep you safe now."

The tension in her heart had eased, and the madman no longer stalked her dreams. Until now. This time when Kristian woke up, there were no loving arms to embrace her. Only darkness and fear. Shivering in the cold, she tried to ignore the panic she was feeling. Nothing helped. When she closed her eyes, his sadistic smile leered at her. When she opened them, she was greeted with a darkness that did nothing but remind her he was once again in control of her life. *God, help me*, she pleaded silently.

Chapter 10

The Volvo groaned as Lewinsky plunked into the seat. His head grazed the top while he wrestled his legs under the wheel. Shaking his head disgustedly, he chided himself for buying such a rinky-dink vehicle. He knew he should have just taken a squad car, but he was still on "rookie probation." When the chief heard he side swiped a pole at the Wendy's drive thru, he'd lost his company wheels. Lewinsky wasn't allowed anywhere near a black and white unless he was a passenger.

Lewinsky flipped the radio on to drown out the ringing in his ears. The chief's papered wife was none to happy to hear that Brody bowed out of their dinner engagement. Chrissy ranted she'd be the only one without an escort, and the ladies would have a field day with her. Especially some broad named Tiffany who, apparently, had nothing better to do than harass the people around her. Blah...Blah...blah...tongues wagging about her...blah...blah...blah. He had tuned her out about mid tantrum. Of course, Chrissy noticed the glazed look on his face and couldn't handle that she wasn't the center of his attention. The wench actually chucked a book at him. Nothing like having a Harlequin Romance nail you right between the eyes. Tears gushing, she'd blubbered something about having his badge removed and stuck "where the rays of the sun would never unearth it."

Talk about a drama queen!! Jeesh, it wasn't like the chief stood her up on purpose. After Chrissy's little display, he was beginning to understand why Brody ran around half cocked all the time. That woman would make anybody a walking time bomb. It was a wonder the chief hadn't gone crazy and wrung her neck. Lewinsky smiled at the thought. The chief's meaty paws squeezing the air out of her until she couldn't screech anymore. He'd be willing to testify that it was completely self-defense. No man in Wyoming would convict him, he was sure of that.

Thumping his hand on the steering wheel, Lewinsky had to force himself to slow down. Twilight was setting in, and the shadows outnumbered the rays of light. When he'd left, Brody was breaking everybody up into surveillance groups. He wanted to be back in time to be a part of the action. If he was lucky, he'd get assigned to Austin's detail. He was the only one on the force who didn't ride him incessantly about his size. Besides, Austin always made sure he was included and didn't send him on those po-dunk gopher missions.

Scanning the countryside, he lazily watched for any movements. The deer were extra frisky this time of night, and he didn't need any fender benders. Out of the corner of his eye, he noticed a set of ruts on the opposite road ditch. They dug into the embankment, and the muddy trail fanned out onto the highway. Judging from the size of the ruts, the driver was in some kind of hurry. Lewinsky raised an eyebrow and couldn't help thinking it seemed strange. Why would someone be off roading at the wilderness preserve? Several thousand acres were set aside last year as a sanctuary for the local wildlife. The garden club had finally gotten some trails finished, so people could have a place to wander through the woods.

He was so intent on eyeballing the tracks, his tires slipped off the pavement. Lewinsky jerked the wheel and over corrected to the left. Back and forth, the car flirted with the ditches before he finally got it straightened out. His heart pounded in his chest, and he decided not to go back to investigate. It was probably just some local kids having a joy ride. He made a mental note to let the chief know later. Right now there were more important things to do, like get in on a manhunt.

With tunnel vision, Lewinsky headed back to the station. Even when his headlights glint off of a windshield, he never slowed down. The car was nestled back in the trees on one of the gravel parking areas. A faint glow illuminated the front seat. The cell phone display read 'Austin' as the muffled sounds of Beethoven drifted through the trees. Caleb's picture was mounted to the display panel, and Kristian's work clothes were strewn in the passenger seat.

Chapter 11

The spoon flew out of her hand, arched towards the ceiling and slammed into the bar behind her. Spaghetti sauce splattered all over the freshly mopped floor, and Gretchen sputtered,

"God D...bless America!"

Caleb's eyes were wide in anticipation. He'd nearly caught her saying the "D" word. With his elephant memory, she'd never live it down.

The sounds of crunching gravel echoed through the kitchen. Someone had come to an abrupt halt outside, and the unexpected noise sent chills down Gretchen's spin. A car door slammed, and the slap of running feet could be heard on the porch.

"What in tarnation is going on out there?" Gretchen demanded. She wasn't expecting anyone one but Kristian. If that was her, then something was seriously wrong. In all the years she'd known her, Kristian never went over 25 miles per hour on the gravel. The girl wouldn't squall a tire if her life depended on it, much less spin out in her own driveway.

Before she could go investigate, the front door slammed open. It slapped against the wall as the hinges bounced. Austin came barreling in, his hair was every which way, and he looked like he'd seen a ghost. Face drawn and eyes frantic, he shouted, "Where's Kristian? Have you heard from her yet?"

It took Gretchen a second to register what she was being asked. She was still in shock by his uncharacteristic entrance. Austin was the epitome of mellow, and his voice never rose above a conversational tone. Why, she'd seen a drunk kick him in the shins and call him every slur known to man. It never even phased him. Anybody else would have shredded the old bum, but Austin was too calm to get drawn into an argument. So, why was he so angry now? A ball of lead was starting to form in Gretchen's stomach. Whatever it was, it couldn't be good.

"I haven't seen hide nor hair of her. Matter of fact, I've been calling her cell phone, and she doesn't answer. That ain't like her, especially when she's running late. Something the matter?"

Austin looked like she'd just punched him in the gut. He sucked in a big breath and put his hands over his forehead. Closing his eyes, he started muttering, "Oh God...oh God...oh God...help me to find her before he does any harm."

From where Gretchen stood, she couldn't be sure whether Austin was moaning or stammering a prayer. One thing was for sure, he was scaring the bejeebas out of her. Her heart started pounding in her chest, and she could feel the little hairs standing up on the back of her neck. Gripping the bar with white knuckles, she forced herself to breathe normally.

Caleb sat silently watching the exchange trying to figure out what the fuss was about. Sometimes, Momma had to work late, but it wasn't anything to throw a fit about. Besides, Momma always said a fit didn't do nothing but get you in trouble. He'd even gotten a butt spanking to prove it, too.

Scooching his chair back, Caleb walked over and tugged on

Austin's pant leg. Startled, he dropped his hands and looked down. Until that moment, Austin hadn't even realized the boy was in the room. He'd been so anxious when he came in to find Kristian, it hadn't registered that little ears might be listening.

With his head tilted back, Caleb looked up at Austin with his eyes full of wonder. Crooking one finger, he motioned for Austin to bend down. If he was going to set the man straight, he needed to be on eye level. Momma always got face to face with him when she told him how it was. Once Austin knelt down, Caleb put his hand on his shoulder and said,

"Austin, being upset ain't gonna bring Momma home no faster." Leaning in, he whispered in Austin's ear. "All's your gonna get is a sore bottom and lots of trouble. I know." He nodded conspiratorially and glanced over his shoulder to see if Gretchen caught any of it. Judging by the hand on her hip, he guessed she had.

"Young man, you need to watch that mouth of yours. You needn't bother Austin with your silly notions. Now, you march yourself in the other room and watch cartoons until we've finished talking." Gretchen's voice had the move-it-or-be-skinned overtone in it.

"But…I haven't finished eating." Caleb stuck his lower lip out and bunched his eyebrows together. Why was it every time he told a grown up the way of things, he had to go in the other room? Nobody made Momma leave the table when she got on to him for throwing a fit. One of these days, he was going to be big and then everybody else would have to 'march' out of his way.

To his utter surprise, Gretchen said, "Well, then, take it with you. Just lay a towel down on the carpet, so you don't spill. Now, move!" He was never, ever allowed to eat in the living room.

Before Caleb turned to go, Austin pulled him into his chest. Wrapping his arms around him, he kissed the top of his head.

"Thanks, buddy. I needed that." Austin pulled back so he could give Caleb a wink. "You better do as Gretchen asked, or she's liable to spank us both."

Caleb graced him with his cockeyed grin and rushed to grab his plate. His sock feet pattered on the floor as he went in the other room. Austin shook his head as he watched him retreat. The boy was already way beyond his years.

Gretchen waited until she heard the television kick on in the other room before she turned back to Austin. As soon as she heard the sounds of Sponge Bob Squarepants, she figured it was safe to continue.

"You mind telling me what the devil is going on? Kristian's missing in action, you come speeding in here like James Bond tires blazing and burst into the house like some kind of whirlwind. Done made me fling spaghetti all over the place and nearly wet my pants. Then, when I tell you I ain't heard from Kristian you started moaning like someone done kicked you in the spleen. What in the hello has gotten into you?"

As rattled as Austin was, he still had to smile over Gretchen's colorful rendition of the evening's events. She sure could turn a phrase when she got upset. Shaking his head, he had a hard time finding the words to answer her. He didn't want to alarm her anymore than he already had, but, by the same token, he didn't want her to do something careless because she didn't know the full story.

Scratching the back of his head, Austin contemplated where to begin. He wasn't sure how much of her past Kristian had given to Gretchen. Before he could speak, Gretchen leaned in and said,

"You're about as bad as Caleb. Would you just spit it out?

Ain't like I'm gonna knock your head off. I might put a little heat to your seat if you don't speed it up though. I'm plum wore out and too aggravated for your lolly gagging."

Ducking his head so she wouldn't see the grin, he answered, "Yes, ma'am. I'll be sure to get right to it." His voice dripped false chagrin, and he put on his best little lost puppy look. Gretchen fired him a look, and he decided he better get to the point, and quick. No wonder Caleb toed the line. That woman had the best do-as-I-say-or-be-smacked look he had ever seen. Huh, and he thought his momma was good with the stink eye.

Clearing his throat, he asked, "Did you happen to see the news this evening?"

"Now, you know I watch the news every night right there on the television behind you. What's that got to do with the price of beans?"

"So, you're aware that an escaped murderer is headed this direction?" Austin cocked his head to the side and raised an eyebrow in a question mark.

"Well…yeah. But…" Gretchen stammered. She shifted her weight, so she could buy some time to think. Surely, Austin didn't think the missing killer had anything to do with Kristian's absence. She was just tied up with some woman who was taking advantage of her kindness. Right? The cloying fingers of uneasiness began to creep into Gretchen's chest.

"Did they give the convict's name or show a picture? I was tied up in the chief's office, so I didn't get to watch."

Gretchen cocked her head back and looked at the border along the kitchen wall. Squinting her eyes a bit, she brought up the image of the killer in her mind. That hawk like nose and those eyes. Something about those eyes, it sent a chill down her spine. Now what was the name they gave. Something Williams. Carl? Cale? No, wait, it was Cole.

Her eyes opened wide in recognition. She suddenly realized why his face was so familiar. Why didn't she see it before? The man had Caleb's eyes. Of course, his were hardened with hatred, but the cobalt coloring was a mirror image of the little boy.

The desire to sit down became overwhelming. Stumbling to the nearest bar stool, she collapsed fanning her face with her hand. Austin rushed to her side and put his arm on her shoulders. Judging from the panic on her face, she must have made the same connection he did. Gretchen tried to force herself to take air in at a normal pace. The harder she tried, the more it ended like a bad Lamaze lesson. Gasping for air, she put her head between her knees to keep from getting light headed. *Of all the times to hyperventilate*, she thought. The last time she had wheezed this hard was when the doctor told her her husband wasn't going to make it. George was her knight in shining armor, and she'd always thought of him as indestructible. Even when they diagnosed him with cancer, she was sure he'd lick it like he did everything else. Why, the man had tangled with a grizzly bear and come out on top. Unfortunately, the cancer took its sweet time, but, in the end, it came out the winner.

Austin stood awkwardly, patting Gretchen's back and trying to comfort her with his presence. The last thing he expected was for old "hard nose" to fall apart on him. All the ladies in town were convinced she wore iron underpants. They joked when they said colder than a witches titty they were referring to Gretchen and her metal brassier. He knew underneath the gruff exterior, she was a very compassionate person. Anyone else would be able to see it if they'd just give her half a chance.

As she worked to inhale and exhale, Austin heard himself saying, "Easy. Calm down. Everything's going to be all right.

You'll see." The thin words hung limp in the air between them. He couldn't even convince himself, so how was he going to calm down an hysterical woman?

His hollow words punched Gretchen in the gut. Wasn't nobody going to mealy mouth her, not even Austin, bless his heart. Nothing she hated more than a simpering female who had to be lied to to spare her feelings. She wanted the truth straight, and Austin dang sure better give it to her. Gretchen pulled herself back together with an internal tongue lashing. Wiping her hand over her face, she ran her fingers along the outline of her mouth. She pinched her lower lip between her thumb and forefinger and let out a long sigh.

"Well, I've embarrassed myself enough for one evening. Here I am blubbering like an idiot, and there are more important things to be worrying about than my own feelings. Now, give it to me straight. No more pussy footing around. I can take it, I swear."

She pulled herself back where she could look Austin in the eye. Her eyes snapped, and she had her jaw set in a no nonsense clamp. Austin was glad Gretchen was back to her old self. As much as he hated to admit it, he needed someone to lean on who fully understood the situation, past and present.

Austin filled her in on the details of the escape and the manhunt initiated by Brody. He omitted the part where the con was looking for a "piece of ass" with his name on it. Gretchen didn't need to know all the graphic information. Hell, he didn't even want to think about it. Kristian was out there somewhere, and her lunatic ex was headed this way. What if he already had her? The thought sent chills down his spine. He'd just have to make sure he found her first.

When he finished talking, Gretchen instinctively walked to the doorway to check on Caleb. He was still sitting cross-legged in the floor with his face propped in his hands. The characters on the screen were talking gibberish and Caleb's laughter rang out as the pink one smacked the yellow one. He sounded so carefree and innocent. *Dear God, don't let anything happen to change that*, Gretchen silently prayed.

Austin's cell phone intruded on the silence between them. Fumbling with his pants pocket he rushed to answer. He had his phone programmed with customized rings for the people who called him. Anyone from the force was set to play "Take Me Out to the Ball Game," his family played jazz and Kristian's played classical. His pocket was definitely singing Beethoven. In his hurry to get the phone open, he nearly hung up.

"Honey, thank goodness you're okay! Where have you been? We've been worried sick." The relief in his voice made the words tumbled out in one big rush.

What he heard next, made his heart constrict and a wave of panic washed over him. It was all he could do to keep from hurling the phone across the room. Rather than the reassuring sounds of Kristian's voice, he was greeted with the gravely sounds of a man.

"Huh, I'm not your honey, and you haven't even begun to see sick, lover boy."

"Where is she?" Austin rasped into the phone. "If you've hurt her..."

"Ah, how quaint, you're worried about the welfare of *my wife*. Maybe you should have done that before you laid your hands on her. You ought to be more worried about yourself and how you're going to explain to *my son* that your affair will cost him a mother."

"She's not your wife, you possessive bastard! I believe the courts relieved her of that sentence around the same time they put you in prison. Now, where is she?"

"Coming from a man whose never been wed. Last time I checked the vows, Kristian agreed to take me as her husband until death do us part. I'm simply going to make sure she honors her word. If she wants out so bad, she needs to pay the price. Surely, as a God fearing man, you can understand the need to stand by what you say?"

"Don't act so high and mighty. You were never a husband to her. Anyone who could abuse a woman the way you did, doesn't deserve the title. For the last time, where is she? This town is crawling with cops. You'll be better off in the long run if you just let her go. The last thing you need is another body on your wrap sheet."

"You wanna know where she is? I'll tell ya. Last time I checked, she was laying about six feet under in a puddle of blood. Couldn't be sure, but I think her chest may have been going up and down when I left her." Cole's sadistic laughter was the last thing Austin heard as the phone disconnected.

Chapter 12

Cole clicked her phone closed and couldn't help laughing at the stupid cop. He obviously had it bad for her. Heck, Kristian's phone had over fifteen missed calls from the guy in the past hour. She was probably still wooing him with her Sunday school charms. All sunshine and innocence until she slipped on the ring. Good for nothing slut! Talk about your false advertisement! She comes on like Pollyanna and then ends up being a two timing whore. The poor sap would have figured it out sooner or later. When he ended her, he'd be doing the old boy a favor.

He slipped Kristian's phone in his pocket and started back through the woods. He had the overwhelming need to hear her beg. Once she found out what he had in store for her precious son, she'd be whimpering. Maybe, if he played his cards right, he could take her for one last drive before he disposed of her. The thought of her luscious mouth and those full breasts made his blood tingle. After all she'd put him through, he deserved to be pleasured at his wife's expense. It wasn't exactly what he had originally planned, but then, nothing was anymore.

He let out a low hiss of breath as he recalled the news

bulletin on the radio. Cole was listening to some classic rock to calm his nerves. The anticipation was more than he could handle. After all this time, he finally had her in reach, and he could hardly contain himself. Leaned back in his chair, he flipped completely backwards when he heard his name come across the local radio station. The FBI had issued an all points bulletin. Cole Williams was believed to be in the Fort Wayne area after killing two prison guards. The police considered him armed and very dangerous.

After a few moments lying on the floor with his feet in the air, Cole registered they were on to him. He figured he had several more days before anyone figured out where he was going. By then he hoped to have things wrapped up and be well on his way to Virginia. He had an e-mail acquaintance he wanted to look up. He'd met her in one of those chat rooms, and she sounded like a real good time.

Those stupid pigs must have gotten someone to squeal on him. Go figure. But, who would rat him out? The only one who knew where he was headed was the bounty hunter he'd hired to find Kristian. With the list of crimes on his record, he would have knocked someone out before he told the FBI anything. Think, man, think. Maybe Frankie had overheard him talking to his informant. The little pock marked weasel would do anything if the price was right.

Ugh. All the time he spent planning and meticulously going over the details. What a waste! Now what was he going to do? Staring up at the water stained ceiling, the thought of walking away crossed his mind. No one knew exactly where he was. If he stayed relaxed, he could probably slip out of town without being noticed. They would comb the town for days, and he'd be well on his way to the other side of the country.

Cole inwardly cringed at the thought of turning tail. Hell no!

He couldn't just let the opportunity slip through his fingers. He'd already contained her which went a lot easier than anticipated. For all intents and purposes, he was way ahead of schedule. Since the damage was done, he would just have to speed up his game plan. Yeah, that's it. Licking his lips, a tinge of excitement shot down his spine and settled in his pants. Pay backs were going to be hellacious.

Putting the essentials in his back pack, he debated whether or not to bring the jeep. He wanted to be able to make a quick escape but didn't want to alert the locals to his whereabouts with the motor running. The need to flee won out. In a matter of minutes, he had the engine revved and headed back towards Kristian.

Keeping to the back roads, he decided to take the scenic route back to his homemade cell. Rather than off roading back to where he'd parked this morning, he decided to come in from the opposite direction. He found an old access road that ran almost parallel with the highway. Grass had grown up down the center of the path and made it nearly impossible to see the pot holes. His headlights danced with the shadows as he bounced along. Before long, the roadway narrowed behind a hill and came to an end at the base of a rock.

Switching the jeep off, Cole figured it was as good a place as any to leave his ride. Tucked back behind the hill, no one would notice it until they got right up on it. With any luck, the cops would stick to checking motels and not come out as far as the wilderness preserve.

Cole slung his backpack over his shoulder and headed towards the underground cave. Judging from what he remembered, it couldn't be much more than a mile or so from where he parked.

After his eyes adjusted to the dark, he could see relatively well. He'd honed his night vision traipsing around in the dark hunting coon. His helmet light was always going out, so he was forced to rely on his own two eyes. Walking briskly, it wasn't long before he happened upon Kristian's car. The gravel parking area was tucked in behind some trees. If he'd veered any further to the north he would have missed it completely.

He hadn't really meant to call anyone when he'd snagged Kristian's phone from the front seat but couldn't resist. When he'd flipped it open, she had nearly twenty missed phone calls. Fifteen were from Austin, and the rest were from home. Lover boy must have been a little obsessive to call that many times. If the man was concerned now, he'd just give him something more concrete to worry about. The no good s.o.b deserved to squirm. Anybody who would take another man's wife and hold her like she was his own made his skin crawl. Her milky skin against his grubby paws, Cole's head pounded at the thought. Austin would pay for his transgressions and so would she. His momma always said it takes two to tango. They both deserved to rot for what they did to him. How dare Kristian betray him and with a cop no less.

Cole's anger fueled his desire to make her suffer before she breathed her last. His feet slapped against last year's fallen leaves. Crunch...reet...crunch...reet, he was past the point of worrying if someone heard him. Dodging tree limbs and sticker bushes, he ignored the pain as the occasional branch slapped him in the face. Jaw set, he only had one thing in mind, and his mouth watered in anticipation.

Chapter 13

Somehow, in the darkness, Kristian's other senses were intensified. The dank smell of mildewing sludge made the insides of her nose tingle. She pinched her nose between her thumb and forefinger to try and ease the irritation. Unfortunately, with her nose closed off she'd made the mistake of breathing through her mouth. Now, her tongue felt heavy with mildew. Blahh, the stuff tasted worse than it smelled. She started coughing as soon as the musty air settled in the back of her throat. The gag reflex took over, and she started dry heaving. Her stomach lurched but was too empty to unload. The last thing she'd had to eat was Gretchen's meat loaf the night before. Work kept her so busy she didn't take the time to eat anymore.

Kristian's sides ached as she strained to get herself under control. Her raspy coughs echoed against the sides of her prison and slammed into her already aching head. In the midst of her struggle, she thought she could hear a thumping in the distance. It was coming from the ground above and was steadily getting closer. Her heart started thumping in her chest as she forced herself to focus on the source of the sound. The best she could tell, it was coming from behind her and was getting louder with each thump. When the dull thud got directly over head, it suddenly stopped.

It wasn't until the sound stopped that she realized she'd been holding her breath. Slowly, Kristian exhaled the pent up air. Tiny needles prodded her lungs as she struggled to let it out quietly. Like it really matter. He already knew where she was. Stay calm, she pleaded with herself. Maybe it was just a passing deer or a really large squirrel. Yeah, that's it. A squirrel that walks on two legs and weighs as much as a man.

Disgusted with herself, Kristian put her hand over her face and willed herself not to scream. The only way she was going to keep her sanity was if she stayed in control of her fears. She would not give him power over her again. Not again. Not after all she'd been through to rid herself of his repulsive memory. A cold chill ran down her spine and settled in the pit of her stomach. To think, she'd actually let that monster touch her.

Leaves rustled above, and the man-made lid started to shift. A shaft of light penetrated the all encompassing darkness. At first, it was the soft gray highlights of the night air. The sounds of someone fumbling around seemed magnified in the quiet. Kristian heard a muffled curse and then a yellow beam slammed her in the face.

"Oh God," Kristian muttered. "Fill me with your peace and keep me safe." She lay as still as possible and tried not to think about him eyeballing her. He had a way of undressing her with his eyes, and it always made her feel violated. Just don't think about it, she told herself. Maybe, if she played dead long enough, he'd go away.

Seconds felt like hours as the light illuminated her eyelids. She could sense him staring at her, and the thought was unnerving. The nerves under her eyes twitched, and her eyebrows seemed to jump under the strain. As if that wasn't enough, the insides of her nose began to tickle with an uncontrollable itch. Why didn't he just go away?

The beam seemed to falter and was no longer pointed directly at her. Through lidded eyes, Kristian tried to figure out what Cole was doing. The flashlight was aimed at the ground above, and she could hear him scrounging around for something. Since he seemed occupied, she took the opportunity to scratch her nose. Lifting her arm off of her thigh, she rubbed until the itch was placated.

Kristian was in the process of resuming her position when the flashlight swung her direction. She barely got her hand laid down on her chest before she was in the spotlight again. Cole couldn't have seen the motion, but he'd have to be blind not to notice the change in position. Dang it. Hopefully, he was too preoccupied to notice.

Waiting for the worst, she willed herself not to flinch. Every muscle tingled with her effort to hold still. Adrenaline pumped to her broken leg and made it throb with each heart beat. Between that and the ache in her head, the pain was nearly unbearable. Easy, girl, easy. He never did pay too much attention to detail, why should now be any different?

Cole focused his attention on the rope ladder he'd fashioned. When he was in scout's, they taught them how to knot a rope so it would be easier to climb. He tied one end around a sycamore tree and planned to drop the other end into the cave. At first glance, Kristian appeared to be unconscious. He couldn't tell if her chest was still moving or not. The shadows played tricks with his eyes, and he needed to get a closer look. She better hope she hadn't died on him. He'd hate to have to take it out on her son if she'd decided to exit before he was ready. Stupid wench.

He threw the rope over the lip of the cave and shined the light down to figure out the best place to climb in. Cole glanced at Kristian in the process but didn't fully register her position. He lowered himself down one knot at a time. When he got half way, it dawned on him something was different. It nagged at him until he decided to aim the flashlight back at her. Flashlight clenched in his left hand while he held on with his right, Cole stared down at Kristian's motionless body. He tilted his head to the side and squinted as he tried to figure out what bothered him. Her leg was still at the same crazy angle, her head lolled to the left as before and her hand...her hand! That was it. It had been laying on her thigh before, and now it was nestled between her breasts almost like an invitation.

So, she thought she could deceive him. Typical, considering she'd lied to him throughout most of their relationship. Huh, she didn't know who she was dealing with now. Prison made him hard and calculating. He'd learned things from murderers and rapists that would make her blood run cold. His lip curled in anticipation as he planted his feet in the mud beside her.

Cole knelt down and his knee barely touched the side of her rib cage. He could feel her heart pounding through her side. Good. She was scared. He'd make sure she didn't forget it, either. Kristian always tried to bluff him with her calm exterior, but deep down she knew who was in control. Before he finished, he wanted her to admit it. Hell, he needed her to.

Gently, he reached over and brushed his thumb against her cheek. He kept his eyes on her face as he slowly traced her full, pouty lips. They quivered slightly under his touch. From there, his finger ran over her chin and down her milky white neck. Her skin was softer than he remembered.

He grinned as he watched her eyes jump behind her eyelids. Cole had to admit, her self control was amazing. How many women would still pretend to be unconscious when they knew the end was coming? Kristian was a smart girl. She knew he wanted blood. Huh, he'd seen it in her eyes this afternoon when she'd run from him. The day they'd sentenced him to prison he'd told her someday he would kill her. She'd been sitting behind the prosecutor when he'd whispered that she and the squall titty would die. The shear horror on her face kept him going when he was behind bars. Every woman was made to be broken, and he was just the man to do it.

Cole fanned his fingers out and fluttered them over her spandex top. In slow motion, he let his fingers rove over the tight material. They explored every inch until they came to rest on the tell tale hand. Gently, he slipped his hand under hers and raised it up to his mouth. With her fingers curved over his, he pressed his lips against the back of her hand. The tenderness in his touch only lasted a second. With a flick of his wrist, he snapped Kristian's fingers backwards making her cry out in pain.

"You conniving little witch. Did you really think you could fool me again?" Cole demanded. He glared at the back of her eyelids. Even though he knew she was awake, she still kept them clamped shut. How quaint, as if not looking at him would make him go away or maybe the blow to the head reverted her back to toddlerhood. As long as they can't see you, you can't see them. She'd look him in the eye for this if he had to pry her lids open with his fingers. Those green eyes were so expressive. He wanted to watch them dance in terror as the end drew near.

"Oh, cut the crap, woman. We both know you're awake, so why don't you just lift those long lashes? I want you to look me in the eye, if you can. Or are you to overcome with shame to look at the man you betrayed?" He taunted her with his voice and a not so gentle tap to the chin. The sarcasm hung in the air like a dense fog.

Kristian swallowed slowly and willed her eyelids not to give in. He could mock her all he wanted, but she wasn't going to let him tell her what to do. She'd done enough bowing and scraping when they were married. Let him throw a tantrum. At this point, she almost wished he'd knock her out and be done with it. Jaw clenched, she stuck her chin out in defiance.

"Be bullheaded if you want. It'll just make it harder on Caleb in the end. The brat's got to be, what, three or four by now? Quite the little man I'm sure with all that pampering you give him. It's a shame I'll have to drag it out since you're unwilling to cooperate. I'd thought to go easy on the boy, seeing as how he's my only son. A quick twist of the neck or even some pills in his pudding to make him go into endless sleep. Guess I'll get to be more creative."

Cole rocked back on his heels to let his words soak in. He'd watched as the color drained from her face. From white to gray in a matter of seconds. Wham bam thank you ma'am and she was once again putty in his hands. Man, it was good to know he still had it.

"Tell me, have you ever let the boy know about his father? Or will I be a complete surprise when I steal him from his bed? Should I make the introductions before I choke the life out of him? I mean, I wouldn't want the little fella to think I was a stranger."

Against her better judgment, Kristian's eyes flew open. The light from Cole's flashlight made her squint. How she loathed that man! Her stomach churned as she took in the smug look on his face. It never failed, no matter how hard she tried he always got his way. Cole managed to finagle things around where she had no choice but to give in. The power hungry mongrel wins again, and Kristian hated that she was the one to give him the victory.

It felt like a bad case of deja-vous. In a matter of minutes, she became the abused wife all over again. It sickened her how quickly she could revert back. It was force of habit to give the man what ever he wanted, to placate him with cooperation. No matter what indignities and pain were suffered, the attention had to remain on her. She had to keep his mind off of Caleb. If that meant losing her self respect, so be it. From the way Cole talked, she wouldn't be needing it much longer anyway.

Cole snorted when he saw those lashes flutter open. Mention the brat and she usually was willing to do as he told her. Uhh, he guessed that was one of the reasons he despised the little cry baby so much. Caleb had more power over her in his short life span, than he ever had.

Looking closer at his wife, he noticed the hatred penetrating those fierce green eyes. Her clenched jaws and steady gaze made him very uncomfortable all of a sudden. He could feel her anger boring a hole in his forehead. Unconsciously, he shifted his weight to ease the tension. Used to be, when she looked at him she stared at his feet afraid to make eye contact. Now, she looked him directly in the eye, and her defiance was written all over her face. Kristian had changed since he'd last held her. Time turned her fear into disgust, and he found it incredibly unnerving.

To hide his discomfort, Cole chuckled half heartedly and said, "Easy Ko-Jack. If looks could kill I'd be a dead man walking. I'm not a doctor or anything, but I'd say your suffering from some serious hostility problems."

Cole walked over to the edge of the cave and traced his hand along a grove. The pebbles in the dirt massaged his callouses and gave him time to think. The nervy wench had gotten to him. His resolve wavered as he tried to think about where he wanted to start. Hell, what was the matter with him? Not an hour ago, he'd been rehearsing in his mind all the things he wanted to tell her before he choked her out. In his more vivid fantasies, he taunted her until she begged forgiveness. She laid herself before him for the taking, and he pleasured her until she chanted his name. Once he had her under his charms, he closed his fingers around her neck until she stopped breathing. He grinned slowly at the recollection.

"If I didn't know any better, I'd say you were in need of a good lay. What's the matter the old copper not able to get it up to the standards you're used to?" Cole adjusted his pants to drive home the insinuation.

Kristian's gaze never faltered, and she refused to grace him with a response. The man was an absolute moron. Testosterone must have settled between his ears making it difficult for him to think outside his pants. He was a relic of the cave man era when men beat their chests and lorded over their women. It was a bad episode of me Dick you Jane. She half expected him to start dragging her around by her hair.

Cole's temper flared, and he had the overwhelming desire to knock that look off of her face. His skin crawled under her gaze and unsettled him. He raised his fist and connected with her mouth. Kristian's head snapped back, and her vision blurred under the force.

"How dare you look at me like that? You're the one who slept around town and made a laughing stock out of me. You and those long legs you wrapped around anyone who gave you the chance. I loved you, damn it. Gave you everything I had, including my heart. Hell, I even tried to knock some sense in you so your son wouldn't have to grow up with a slut for a momma. You asked for everything you got. So, don't give me that look like you think I'm some kind of monster. All I did was what needed to be done. Can't you see that?"

Cole's anger made his voice shake and his eyes snap. As he spoke, he paced back and forth in the tiny enclosure. Back and forth, back and forth, he only turned when his toes slammed into one wall forcing him back towards the other. The more he moved, the angrier he became. Why couldn't she see that he was the victim here? He didn't ask for her to break their wedding vows and flaunt his role as the head of the household. If she'd only obeyed like she was supposed to none of this would have happened.

In the silence that followed, Kristian reached a new level of understanding. So, that was it. All those nights dodging fists and nursing bruises. Here she thought he just needed a punching bag. He'd actually convinced himself she'd cheated on him. What made it worse, he thought he had every right to beat her for it. The man was on a power trip because his ego was wounded. Why hadn't she seen it before? She'd been so wrapped up in avoiding the pain she hadn't taken the time to figure out why he was swinging. Not that it made much difference now.

As she watched him fidget, Kristian could feel him losing control. His sanity teetered on the edge of no return. When he first touched her, she could feel the calculate malice in his fingers, but now he seemed so unsure of himself. The shadows deepened the scar on his face and played tricks with his eyes. They flickered under the low light making them bulge around his hawk like nose. She couldn't help noticing how his nostrils flared each time he took a ragged breath. Maybe, just maybe, if she could keep him unbalanced she'd be able to make him forget why he'd come down here.

Kristian maintained her scowl and slowly licked her lips. With as much confidence as she could muster, she said,

"Are you trying to convince me or yourself?"

Her voice was barely above a whisper, but Cole's head snapped back like she'd decked him. He stopped in his tracks and whirled to face her. The hatred in his stance was unbelievable, yet his eyes seemed to recoil from the question. On instinct, he'd pulled his arm back to connect with her jaw, but something kept him from swinging. It was almost like an invisible hand was keeping it in mid air.

Kristian's glare remained steady, but her insides were starting to turn to Jell-O. She wanted to push him to the point where he couldn't function, but she didn't want him to snap before he got there. Predators under great stress either became more deadly or cracked under the pressure. Kristian was really hoping for the latter.

Cole sputtered but couldn't find the words to respond. Kristian took the opportunity to continue.

"You and I both know you are the only man, and I use the term loosely, I have ever been with. To me, you'll never be anything more than a power hungry monster. From the day we were married, you wanted to control my every movement. How I dressed, who I talked to, when I was allowed to go out and when I didn't comply, you hit me. Must make you feel real tough when you leave marks on a woman half your size. Maybe I should let you in on a little news flash. You've twisted reality in your own mind so you can justify your abusive behavior. It's what we sociologists refer to as rationalization."

Kristian realized she'd gone to far when Cole let out a roar of frustration. His voice echoed off the walls as he lunged at her. In one fluid motion, he had his hands wrapped around her throat and dropped a knee in her stomach. Cole's body weight hit her full force knocking the air out of her. She'd barely managed a gasp when his fingers started to tighten.

The panic on her face made Cole's adrenaline pump. What

made her think she could quote her textbook crap at him, anyway? He wasn't just some half cocked, illiterate brute. He was a man. A husband who had been wronged by the wife he had loved more than anything. Ugh...how dare she try to make him feel like an animal? Kristian deserved all she got and then some. Hell, they used to stone women to death who did half the crap she had. Wasn't that in that precious Bible she used to push at him all the time?

Cole felt her flailing beneath him, and leaned down to whisper in her ear.

"I could end you, but, somehow, I don't think justice would have been served. Such a conniving wench. Even when you know you've been had, you still try to manipulate me with your mind games. Not this time, honey."

Cole loosened his grip and leered over her. Kristian gasped for air and instinctively rubbed her fingers on her neck. She could feel the tender bruises where his fingers dug into her flesh. *Dear Lord, forgive me for taunting him,* Kristian inwardly prayed. *Please just let him get this over with if it be your will. Amen.*

He shifted his leg to where he straddled her suggestively. Kristian felt his lips brush against her ear as he said,

"I want you to watch him die first. Then, if you're lucky, I'll let you end your misery." With his body on top of hers, Cole laughed sadistically. Kristian could feel his pleasure vibrating against her. Cole flicked his tongue against her earlobe and chuckled, "You need to know what it feels like to lose a son."

Chapter 14

He didn't really need the tooth pick, he just liked to roll it around in his mouth when he was thinking. Terrance was still mulling over all the information he'd gleaned from Austin. The man stormed out of the chief's office like a man with blood hounds on his tail. Brody was so flabbergasted at his behavior, his jaw nearly scrapped the floor. One minute they were looking at a picture of the wanted man, and the next they were looking at Austin's backside on his way out the door.

Brody thought the FBI was full of crap when they said the killer came to their little town. But, after the way Austin reacted, he started having second thoughts. He was the most level headed cop on the force. Not like Lewinsky who went off half cocked anytime someone said boo. Austin was steady, reliable. So, why did he race out of here mumbling something about Kristian? It didn't add up.

While Brody stomped around mulling things over, Terrance leaned back and let his investigative mind go to work. He didn't know much about the woman Austin was involved with. From what he remembered, Kristian was a fine specimen of female perfection. Those pouty lips and sashaying hips made all the guys want more. She left the men panting and the wives stewing when she'd shown up at the policeman's ball. In full evening attire, her hair framed her heart shaped face. From the look of it, she hadn't taken much time to priss, but, umm, did she look good. Her plum colored dress clung in just the right spots even though it was a relatively modest design. It showed off her shapely chest and silhouetted those long legs. Not to mention the fact that it set off her emerald eyes. Even from a distance, those eyes could set your heart thumping.

When she'd first come in, Terrance had been listening to his date drone on about what a deal she'd gotten on her sling back shoes. The sales clerk was smitten with her beauty and let her have them half price. Yadda, yadda, yadda. He'd only brought the self centered twit because his sister said she was perfect for him. Apparently, the only standards his dear sweet sister had was that the woman was single and still breathing. She'd nearly talked his ear off, and they'd only been there twenty minutes.

Kristian's entrance nearly cost him a rib. Without realizing it, he'd been openly staring at her as she made her way across the room with Austin. Felicia stopped mid sentence when she realized he wasn't giving her his full attention. Following his gaze, she jabbed him in the ribs with her elbow. She didn't come to this ball to watch her date ogle some other Cinderella. Why, it took her nearly four hours to get ready for heaven's sake!

Her sharp jab and raised eyebrow brought Terrance back to reality. Judging by the angry scowls on the other women's faces, he wasn't the only one gawking. Even the married men had a sheepish look on their faces like they'd been caught with their hand in the candy jar. What made it even more refreshing was that Kristian continued across the floor completely oblivious to the stir she was making. She had her arm tucked under Austin's and looked completely enthralled in what he was saying. Damn, he was one lucky man.

Austin eventually spotted him in the crowd, and the couple made their way over to Terrance's table. Felicia seemed rather icy about the whole situation, but then she was so jealous it was to be expected. Throughout the evening, Terrance was impressed with Kristian's warm, personable demeanor. She engaged in the conversation but always managed to avoid talking about herself. If things got to close to her, she'd steer things back to a safer subject. She did it with such ease that most of the others probably didn't even notice.

He'd found it so intriguing at the time, he cornered Austin the next day to see if he could fill in the missing gaps. After a little nudging, Austin finally told him that Kristian had been married previously, and it was a rather abusive relationship. He'd been unwilling to give him any of the gory details. The lack of information made Terrance believe the man must have been horrible for no one to mention him. What kind of a moron would hit a woman as fine as Kristian? If he had a girl like that to come home to, he'd probably be catering to her every whim.

As soon as Austin muttered her name after seeing the mug shot, Terrance put two and two together. The man they were after must be the abusive ex-husband. If he was willing to kill two prison guards to get out, he would have no problem shedding more blood when he found Kristian. No wonder Austin went out of here the way he did.

As he watched the chief sputtering, he figured he was oblivious of the situation. He was still looking for a murderer who supposedly came this direction. Brody just wanted to go through the motions of a manhunt but couldn't believe that they would actually uncover anyone. Terrance would be glad when the FBI agents arrived. At least they would take the search seriously. Maybe then they could contain the bastard before he found Kristian.

Disgusted with Brody, Terrance told him he'd go find Austin, and they would start their part in the search. He wanted to let the chief in on reality but decided he'd better wait until he'd talked to Austin first. Maybe, on an off chance, his assumption might be wrong. Why worry Brody unnecessarily? Besides, as high strung as he was he'd just bumble it up anyway. In order to stalk a killer, one had to stay calm and collected. Over the years, Terrance learned to stifle his nerves. As long as he didn't get riled, his instincts usually led the way. His buddies used to ask him if he had a sixth sense or something. When he was in his groove, he could get one step ahead of the killer and trip him up. It was exhilarating.

If the beads of sweat were any indication, Brody was already anything but calm. The man was giving himself an ulcer, and he didn't even know the half of it. He'd probably go into cardiac arrest if he knew the killer really was in Fort Wayne and stalking one of his upstanding citizens. The way those veins were bulging in his temples, Brody was due for an explosion at any time.

Terrance commandeered a squad car and headed towards the edge of town. He typically took his motorcycle, but then, he usually flew solo. Hopefully, he could get Austin to jump in with him. If that lunatic was after Kristian, his driving would undoubtedly be impaired.

According to his calculations, Austin probably made a break for Kristian's house. With any luck he found her and was just trying to secure the area. Knowing Mr. Casanova, he wouldn't leave until he was certain his woman and child were well taken care of. Hell, if he had a woman that fine, he'd be staked out on her doorstep. Better yet, he'd hold her on his lap so he could keep track of her until the danger passed. Terrance grinned at the thought.

From what he heard around town, Austin's presence wouldn't be necessary. Kristian's live in nanny was a direct decedent of Atilla the Hun. The woman had ice in her veins and could drop a fly at forty yards just by glaring it to death. She was more protective of her employer and offspring than any watch dog. If Mr. Cole Williams tried to show up unannounced, Gretchen would probably have him singing soprano in a matter of minutes. All it would take is one blow of the rolling pin right below the belt. The woman wielded that thing like it was a machete. Most of the area salesmen quit visiting Kristian's house during the day for fear of getting their heads knocked off.

Once he left the city limits, Terrance found himself scanning the countryside. He'd slipped back into his role of diligent investigator with relative ease. The first thing on the agenda was to try and think like the predator. Where would he go to stay hidden in a small town like Fort Wayne. With a population of ten thousand, the likelihood of going unnoticed was slim to none. Most everybody knew everybody else since several generations of the same families all lived within walking distance of each other. He'd eventually run into someone who'd spot him as a stranger. The "bad" side of town had several seedy motels. They didn't usually ask too many questions, but it would still be a risk. It would require registration and contact with the public. Even if he registered under false name, it would still leave an unwanted paper trail.

Before he could run through all of his options, Terrance pulled into Kristian's driveway. Austin's car was parked cockeyed and the driver's door was still standing open. He could hear the beep, beep of the car's protest as soon as he turned off the engine. The front door was standing open, and he could see the staircase through the screen door.

He shut the car door on the way passed. Without that distraction, he could hear muffled sounds from inside. As he got closer, the sounds became rather disturbing. He could make out the television in the background, but he could also hear the muffled sounds of a woman crying. Not just one of those weepy cries. It was more of a desperate wail than anything else. The cry reminded him of the mother who'd just found out her son had been murdered. Maybe it was coming from the television, but Terrance didn't really think so. The background music remained very bubbly, so the sound didn't quite fit in. The contrast was too strange, even for a cartoon.

When his boots hit the front step, he heard a muffled gasp from the kitchen. He reached his hand up to hit the door bell, but the sounds of little feet slapping the floor distracted him. Before he could hit the button, he saw Caleb skid around the corner hollering, "Mommy!!"

His stocking feet sent him sliding on the hard wood floor. He didn't actually look up to see who was standing at the door until he fell backwards on his bottom. The disappointment was tangible when he saw Terrance in the doorway.

Lip out, he muttered, "Oh, it's just you." He stood up and gingerly rubbed his bottom. His hair was disheveled, and his face was covered in red sauce. If the red stains on his shirt were any indication, he'd just sucked down some serious spaghetti.

Terrance tipped his hat and said, "Well, I'm happy to see you, too. I drove all this way out here to find somebody to test my handcuffs on, and you give me the cold shoulder. I'm rather insulted."

He shook his head and pursed his lips to emphasize his hurt feelings. The change in Caleb was instantaneous. His blue eyes danced, and he bounced eagerly from one foot to the other. He'd been begging Austin to let him try on his handcuffs, and he wouldn't let him. Something about handcuffs not being a toy and he might hurt his wrists if he wasn't careful. Sounded like a bunch of smoke big people used to keep little guys from having fun.

"Ya mean it, Terrance? Ya really mean it?" Caleb clapped his hands together in anticipation. Oh, boy, now he could be like a real sheriff. His teddy bear could be the bad guy, and he'd haul him in. Yeah, buddy!!

Terrance reached for his cuffs about the time Austin rounded the corner. Before he could hand them over, Austin was standing next to the boy. Caleb jammed his hands in his pockets lickety split and shook his head. The last thing he wanted was to get Terrance in trouble. Austin might think he put Terrance up to giving him his handcuffs. That would surely get his own butt paddled. Gretchen said if one adult says no then he convinced another one to do it for him, he would be guilty. Caleb couldn't recollect off hand what he would be guilty of, but in Gretchen's world guilty meant hand meets rear. That was good enough to keep him from wanting to try it.

Oblivious of Caleb's sudden change, Terrance dangled the handcuffs in front of him.

"Well, are you going to check them for me, or what?"

Caleb's eyes got big, and he looked up to see if Austin was listening. He had red rims under his eyes, and one eyelid seemed to be twitching. Uh oh, he must really be mad if his eye was jumping around like that. Sometimes, Gretchen's left eye did the same thing when he asked her to many questions.

Glancing between the men, Caleb was at a loss. Terrance was smiling and wiggling the coveted handcuffs while Austin stared off into space. Taking his chances, he slowly reached out and grabbed hold of the shiny metal. They were cold to the touch and heavier than he expected. Still waiting for the other foot to fall, he held them at arms length giving them the once over with his eyes.

Tousling the boys hair, Terrance said, "Why don't you go in the other room and test them? You'd be doing me a favor. I was thinking about hauling in a bad guy tonight, but I need to be sure they're going to hold up to the strain."

Caleb stood still and stared up at Austin. Did he dare go in the other room or should he just give them back before Austin got upset? He'd never seen him look so aggravated before. Frozen with indecision, his jaw dropped open when Austin said, "That sounds like a good idea to me. Just leave Rascal out of it. The poor dog doesn't need any more excitement today."

"Whoopee!! I can't wait to go arrest my bear. Don't worry, I'll make sure I tell him to remain silent and all that stuff!!"

Caleb couldn't believe his luck. Twice in one night he'd gotten away with things that would ordinarily have been forbidden. First, Gretchen let him eat in the living room, and now Austin was letting him play with handcuffs. As much as he missed his momma, maybe she should be late more often. He pealed out around the corner and nearly tripped over a sleeping Rascal. The dog looked up warily and followed Caleb's movement across the room. Content that the kid wasn't after him, he rolled over and closed his eyes.

As soon as he was out of earshot, Terrance stated flatly, "We need to talk." Austin nodded his assent and motioned him towards the kitchen.

Gretchen still sat motionless on the barstool. She'd been dropped into a nightmare and kept waiting to be woke up. She had the overwhelming desire to pinch herself. The only thing holding her back was the fear that she would feel it making everything an undeniable reality.

The men walked in and sat down at the kitchen table.

Gretchen's stupor finally broke when she saw Terrance. These men were her guests, and her role as hostess kicked in. She needed something to keep her mind occupied, and serving a meal to a hungry man was something she knew how to do. Her heels banged on the floor with new purpose as she got down from her perch. She clickety clacked to the cabinet for some plates and dished up two helpings of spaghetti. Without hesitation, Gretchen plopped the steaming plates in front of the men and went on a quest for utensils. The motions made her feel better and kept her mind off of the terrible things that monster insinuated.

Terrance watched as Austin pushed the food around his plate and waited for the man to start explaining. As good as everything looked, they didn't have time to be sitting around eating while a killer was on the loose. When someone's life hung in the balance, time became the enemy. Each precious minute put them further away from apprehending the demon before he did any serious harm. Judging by Caleb's welcome, Kristian was still unaccounted for. If they didn't get to her before Cole, it might mean just another homicide investigation. He didn't have the energy or the patience for that.

"Look, I know the man we're searching for is Kristian's abusive ex-husband. Caleb made it plain that she hasn't made it home yet. From the look on your face, you know what kind of danger she could be in. If we're going to find her before he does, you've got to tell me everything."

Austin's head snapped up when he heard Terrance refer to the escaped convict as Kristian's ex. He raised his eyebrow in question but never voiced it. What difference did it make how he figured it out? The shock was short lived as the dreadful sense of loss washed over him again. He'd failed her. He'd promised he'd keep her safe from harm, that the past couldn't hurt her anymore. Yet, here he sat and the enemy had her. Her nightmares were coming true, and she was all alone.

"Cole already has her," Austin's voice choked with emotion, and the anguish on his face made Terrance cringed. Surely, he hadn't heard him right. How could he be so certain, when they'd only just found out about the man hunt? Before he could question him, Austin continued,

"He just called me from Kristian's cell phone." Austin quickly filled him in on the conversation. When he got to the part about her being six feet under, Terrance had to grasp his arm to keep him from tipping out of the chair.

Terrance kept one hand on Austin and scratched his chin with the other. The man sounded like a sadistic bastard who loved to play games. If that were the case, he would string this out as long as possible. The thrill came from the hunt and toying with his prey. He fit the profile of the obsessive killer who would drag out the murderous foreplay to prolong his own enjoyment. Death was merely the end result, not the point of the game.

"She's not dead, Austin." The calm certainty in Terrance's voice, made Austin look up. Through blurry eyes, he tried to focus on the other man's face. Terrance looked him right in the eye and waited for his words to sink in.

Austin wanted to believe him, oh God, did he want to believe him. But, what made him so sure? The monster had her, and he already had a number of bodies under his belt. Besides, Cole had made it very plain he had no qualms hurting a woman. Sending Kristian to her grave would be no more traumatizing to him than sending her to the emergency room.

That voice still echoed in his head. 'Six feet under...six feet under.' It was so cold, distant...like the man had permanently separated himself from sanity. They were dealing with a beast of prey, not a human being.

Terrance watched as Austin struggled to accept his statement. Austin's eyes pleaded with him to make it believable. He looked like a drowning man who was just inches from grasping a life rope he couldn't see. Flailing and bobbing in the waves, he needed a glimmer of hope to help him find his way to safety.

"He wouldn't kill her, Austin. At least not yet. It's too early in the game. From what I've gathered about the man, he's a control freak. Cole wants to be the absolute power over someone which, in this case, is Kristian. He needs someone to manipulate in order to feel like he's the man in charge. His ego needs stroking after all that time in prison. Cole gains nothing, if he takes her out now. Think about it, when she dies, the power trip is over. He's only just gotten her under his thumb. If I were him, I'd drag it out so I could enjoy the ride."

Austin mulled it over a minute. What he said made sense. Cole probably would try to lord it over Kristian as long as possible. Which meant, she was still alive. When his mind opened up to the idea that she wasn't dead, the tension in his neck started to ease. She's not dead, and if she's not dead then there was still hope that she could be saved. Of course, the relief was short lived. Kristian may still be alive, but the sadistic bastard would be making her wish she wasn't.

Austin stood straight up and his chair skittered backwards. With both hands on the table, he leaned toward Terrance and nearly shouted, "We've got to find her, NOW! She can't handle another night like the last one, it would kill her."

In his haste, he nearly ripped Terrance out of his chair on his way around the table. His only thought was to get a move on. He had no idea where they were going to start, but the adrenaline made it impossible to hold still. Time kept ticking by and the longer they sat around talking about it, the less likely they would find Kristian before the damage was done.

With some effort, Terrance managed to get his elbow free. Austin had his fingers clamped around it and attempted to use it to propel him out the door. He turned so he could see Austin's face and said, "Now, wait just a minute. Before you run out of here half cocked, I need to know that you can handle this. You have to be a cop first and foremost. That means you don't let your personal interest cloud your judgment. I can't be out there with someone who is going to jeopardize the search because he's too close to the situation. I've been through man hunts before, and it is stressful enough without adding extra baggage to the investigation."

The harsh tone made Austin realize how crazy he must sound to Terrance. One minute he was crying and the next he was ready to knock down the door to start the investigation. It wouldn't do Kristian a bit of good if he let his emotions take over. He took a deep breath and held the air in his lungs until they ached. As he exhaled, he silently prayed. *Dear Lord, grant me the strength and wisdom needed to handle the search. Put your loving arms around Kristian and keep her safe until we can find her. Amen*

When he finished, his eyes shone with a new inner confidence. He may not be able to do it alone, but God would make sure he kept himself in check. Austin nodded is head,

"I can do this. You just tell me where to start, and I'm with you."

The calm in Austin's voice sounded like the man Terrance knew. He'd done a complete turn around in a matter of seconds. That must have been one hell of a breathing exercise.

Satisfied that Austin had himself in check, Terrance said,

"First, we need to get a hold of the chief and let him know what's going on. Last time I checked, Brody was still convinced we were looking for a man who wasn't even in this area. Nothing personal, but I get the impression that he doesn't know much about murder investigations. With any luck, the FBI will be there by now, and they can help us out. We need to get a tap on your phone and the one in the house here just in case he calls again."

"Okay, then what?" Austin replied.

"I think you and I'll go for a drive to see if we can find Kristian's car. It'll give us a starting point to search from. On the way, I want you to fill me in on everything you know about Cole Williams and his relationship with Kristian. Maybe it'll give me a clue as to who we're dealing with."

Austin swallowed hard and nodded. It was hard enough hearing the story from Kristian, but to have to retell it tonight was going to be horrendous. Remembering the past only provoked images of what could be happening in the present. At least this time, Caleb wasn't in any danger.

The thought of Caleb made him remember what Cole had said to Kristian the day he was sentenced. He'd threaten to make her and her son pay. If he already had Kristian, he may be on the prowl for Caleb.

"Terrance, I think we need to have the chief send some guys out to keep watch over Gretchen and Caleb. I don't want to take any chances that the bastard would come after our boy."

Terrance caught Austin's possessive referral to Caleb. He hadn't even realized he'd referred to the boy like he was his own son. Somehow, it didn't seem out of place coming from Austin. He'd probably been more of a father to that kid than the biological. That monster was nothing more than a sperm donor.

"Good thinking. I'll have them send someone out. In the mean time, why don't you jump in with me. We'll leave your squad car here, so it looks like the house is being covered. It shouldn't take more than ten or fifteen minutes for them to get out here."

Austin hesitated. He hated to leave them alone, for any length of time. It would only take a few minutes for things to go wrong. But then, he didn't really have fifteen minutes to spare. Right now, Kristian was the one in immediate danger. He'd be doing her more good out looking, than sitting here baby sitting until back up arrived.

"All right. Just let me go tell Gretchen what's going on."

At some point during Austin and Terrance's conversation, Gretchen had wandered in to watch cartoons with Caleb. He sat snuggled up to her on the couch wearing a felt cowboy hat and matching boots. His teddy bear sat handcuffed to his arm and he was completely enthralled in an episode of Bonanza. Hoss and Little Joe were wrestling with an ornery calf. Gretchen, ordinarily a big fan of the western, only had eyes for the cowboy in her arms. She absently stroked his cantankerous hair with her thumb.

Gretchen looked up when Austin walked in the room, and he could see the tears glistening on her cheeks. She didn't even bother to brush them away as she eyed him expectantly.

"Terrance and I are going to go look for Kristian. Brody is going to send some guys out to keep an eye on the place. They should be here in the next ten or fifteen minutes. Keep the doors locked and don't open the door to anyone who isn't an officer. All right?"

Gretchen bit her lower lip and nodded slightly. She knew if she tried to speak her voice would give away her emotion. All she needed was for Caleb to catch on that she was rattled. The kid would be nonstop questions, and she knew she wouldn't be able to lie to him. At four, he was already a human lie detector. Caleb could sense when you weren't being straight with him, and he took it personally. He could look at you with those big blue eyes and make you feel worthless for trying to slide one passed him. Gretchen just wasn't up to it tonight.

As Austin turned to go, Caleb said, "Hey, Austin, how come you gotta go find momma? Did she get lost?"

Austin froze. How was he supposed to answer that one? His chest constricted, and he could feel the perspiration coming up on his nose. Nothing like a point blank question to make your hands sweaty and your legs shaky. Especially when you didn't have a good answer. It was worse than being singled out in class when you were trying to hide from the professor.

With his back still to the child, he cleared his throat and said, "Well...we just wanted to make sure she hasn't run into any trouble." Even to Austin, his answer didn't sound too convincing. The hollow ring made his stomach churn. Maybe Caleb wouldn't catch on.

"What kind a trouble? She's not in time out is she? Momma's usually pretty good. 'Cept for that one time when she said the 's' word after she stubbed her toe. She didn't know'd I was behind her, but she was real sorry after she done it. That wouldn't make her late would it? Saying the 's' word?"

The innocence in his words choked Austin up. It didn't help that he could feel those little eyes on his back. Two lasers piercing his heart from behind. They prodded him to turn around and face the boy. Every muscle cringed with the desire to run away and pretend he hadn't heard the question. But, deep down, he knew Caleb had a right to know what was going on. At least, in part.

"Buddy, that's not the kind of trouble I'm talking about. Your mom hasn't done anything wrong. She...well... someone...She's gotten tied up on her way home. Terrance and I are going to see if we can help her out."

Ugh, Austin groaned inwardly. When it came right down to it, he couldn't bring himself to do it. He couldn't tell Caleb his psychotic father had his mother prisoner, and they needed to find her before he killed her. Somehow, the words just wouldn't come. With any luck, Caleb wouldn't ever have to know. No child deserves to live with something like that.

Caleb thought about it for a minute and asked, "Ahh, ohh. I thought she know'd better." He shook his head solemnly. "When someone gets to a three, you're 'posed to listen. Who tied her up?"

Austin raised an eyebrow at Gretchen. Would this inquisition never end? And what in the world was Caleb talking about anyway? A three? His head ached, and he really needed to get out of here. The walls were starting to close in on him. If the air got any thinner, he'd probably pass out.

"Honey…" Austin began, halfheartedly. Before he could finish, Terrance interrupted.

"Hey, Buddy? I need some help. You know anybody around here with big muscles?"

Instantly, Caleb was up on his knees in a muscle man pose. With his right arm curled up and his left arm turned down, he flexed with all his might. He stuck his tongue out and bit down for extra affect.

"Whew, those must be the biggest muscles I've seen in a while. You think you can keep track of my handcuffs for me while we're gone? Austin and I need to roll, but I'm still not sure my cuffs are working right."

"Oh, boy, can I!! Did you hear that, Gretchen? I get to watch the handcuffs. Whoopee!! You wanna play cops and robbers? You be the bad guy, and I'll cuff ya? Please, please, please?"

In all the excitement, he forgot about his game of twenty questions. Austin mouthed a thank you to Terrance, and the two turned to walk out the door.

"Hey, Gretchen, I'll leave the key to those cuffs on the counter. The way it sounds, you may be needing them!"

Terrance hollered over his shoulder on the way through the kitchen. He flipped the key on the bar as they passed, and it skid underneath a used napkin.

Gretchen listened to the front door slam and heard the click of the dead bolt catching in the latch. Her nerves twitched in anticipation. She was now officially alone with Caleb. Even though she knew officers would be there shortly, she couldn't stop her heart from thumping faster. Fortunately, Caleb had other things to worry about besides her. Bonanza was forgotten as he strutted with the prize Terrance left. His John Wayne swagger brought a smile to her lips. For a moment, everything was the way it was supposed to be. Caleb lost in play, her getting caught up in his imagination. Any second now, Kristian would be walking through the door to complete the family circle. Gretchen swallowed a sob. If only it were that easy.

Chapter 15

Man did life stink when you were a step below pond scum in the food chain. Lewinsky slouched lower in his chair and groaned over his bad luck. His little trip to talk to Ms. Prissy cost him his chance to get in on the action. When he got back to the station, everyone had already scattered to their respective duties. Place looked like a graveyard. The only guys left were Brody and the paper pushers.

He'd bounced in hoping for a chance to work with Austin, but, rumor had it, he'd blown out of here like a house a fire. Chairs flying this way and hair going every which way, he'd left Brody talking to his backside. Mel, a man older than dirt, claimed to have seen it all. He'd been putting away some paperwork when Austin blew past. Why, to hear him tell it, he nearly bowled him over muttering something under his breath.

Lewinsky wasn't so sure how credible his story was. The old dude should have retired years ago, but he still hung around filing paperwork and answering the dispatch. Said it made him feel useful. Truth be known, somewhere under all those wrinkles lived one of the best old school investigators. He slapped handcuffs on bad guys long before forensic science hit the scenes. He'd hit his prime back when it took savvy and persistence to find the perpetrator, not a piece of hair or a drop of blood. Mel had a knack for profiling a killer. He used to sit at the crime scene absorbing details until he could recreate the murder in his own mind. From the positioning of the body down to the weapon used, he sensed the type of person involved. Once the image formed in his mind, Mel could ferret out the motive and more often than not, he caught his man. Time may have reduced his body to a desk job, but his mind still worked like a steel trap.

Lewinsky drummed his fingers against his desk as he glared at the chief's glass cubical. The man sat with his back to his desk and the light reflected off his bald spot. Brody told him to sit at his desk until otherwise notified. He'd been officially put in time out. The grumpy broad called in and tattled on him for his lack of interest. Apparently, when she speaks everyone's supposed to listen even if she is rattle brained. She sure had the chief snowballed. The old man wasn't fooling anybody with is tough talk around the water cooler. He'd heard the man yes dearing on the phone when the hag called in. Sounded like a whipped dog. If she'd asked him to roll over, he'd have cleared his desk to comply. The minute she'd hung up, Brody lowered the boom on Lewinsky. Something about being demoted to full time gopher. He would not be allowed to do any type of official police work until further notice. Further notice meant when the lower regions of Hades froze over or when the wife gave her blessing. Both not likely to happen in the next twenty four hours.

What a waste of his talents, Lewinsky thought. They finally see some action out here in dulls-ville, and he's stuck behind a desk. Maybe, when the Feds showed up, he'd get recruited to do something besides hold his chair down. Like, head up a search party or help with a road block. He could take the agents around and show them the layout of the town. Brody'd be sorry when they saw how he was holding him back. All he needed was the right opportunity. Just one chance and he'd make them all see. He didn't join the force so he could be the butt of all the jokes. If he'd wanted that he could have stayed at home working in his father's charcoal factory. Suddenly, the phone rang in the chief's office, and Brody whirled around to grab it. Lewinsky tensed at the sound and couldn't help laughing when the phone cord got tangled around Brody's chair. It was already on the fifth ring by the time he unwound himself enough to answer.

The cubicle was too thick for Lewinsky to make out what he was saying. It was like watching a movie that somebody muted. He started out standing up, but he slowly sank into his chair as the color drained from his face. It went from the usual beet red to an ashy gray. His mouth flapped, and his eyebrows raised in question. The eyelids clamped shut, and his free hand flew up to his mouth. Apparently, the answer wasn't a good one. If Lewinsky didn't know any better, he'd say the man was about to spew.

Brody nodded his head a few times and then dropped the phone. It missed the cradle and slumped to the floor. The cord snapped and the receiver bounced around like a bunge jumper gone wild. The chief didn't even bother to pick it up. He just sat staring straight ahead. His chin rested on his thumbs, and he had his fingers steepled up over his nose. Glassy eyed, he appeared to be looking directly at Lewinsky. Lewinsky didn't know whether to run now or later. Ten to one the Mrs. called back to try to get his badge taken away and stuck where the sun didn't shine. She must have laid it on thick, judging from the greenish tinge to Brody's complexion.

Before Lewinsky could make up his mind which way to go, he heard his name shouted over the silence.

"Lewinsky! Get in here." His name sounded choked. Either Brody swallowed a sob, or his anger cut off his air supply. He'd been known to throw tantrums where he nearly hyperventilated with rage. When he got that bad, Austin usually helped him calm down. Lewinsky swallowed hard. Austin wasn't here to curb his temper now, he'd have to face him alone.

In route to the office, Lewinsky stumbled over a loose shoe string. With one foot pinning the wayward string down, he lost his balance. His thigh clipped the corner of Terrance's desk, knocking him the opposite direction. It took several run steps to get himself righted. Fortunately, he didn't fall, but he still felt like a royal donkey. He glanced behind him to see if anyone else had noticed his blunder. Mel looked him dead in the eye and shook his head disgustedly. He'd seen more grace from a pregnant hippo.

When he reached Brody's door, his palms were sweaty. He clamped on the brass knob, and his hand slipped leaving a greasy hand print on the glass. Color rushed to his cheeks as he quickly used his handkerchief to wipe it off. It took both hands for Lewinsky to grasp the handle and let himself into Brody's office.

Staring at his feet, he half expected to be greeted with a tongue lashing. Brody never had much tolerance for his clumsiness and always let him know it with a string of profanities. However, the only thing that met him was silence. The seconds seemed like hours as he waited for the other foot to fall. The chief never bellowed for him to come to his office unless he had a mouth full to say.

When nothing was said, Lewinsky slowly raised his eyes from the floor to see what the hold up was. Maybe the man had finally ruptured that vein in his head or a merciful God had rendered him silent.

Lewinsky wasn't prepared for what he saw. Brody looked through him with a tear on his cheek. The wrinkles etched craters for it to slither down. He seemed broken down and...old. Funny, Lewinsky had never thought of him as anything but a tyrant. Brody commanded with an iron fist and struck fear into rookie cops everywhere. So, why did he look like he was now ready for the old folks home? Apprehension settled in the pit of his stomach as he made his way over to a chair. He didn't think his legs could hold him up any longer.

The chair let out a whoosh of air when Lewinsky sank into it. Brody brought his eyes into focus and seemed startled to see Lewinsky sitting there. He raised his palm and pushed it against the center of his forehead. The lines in his forehead parted to make room, and he heaved a sigh of submission.

"Lewinsky, we've got a problem...disaster, really, on our hands. As much as I hate to do it, I'm going to have to send you out. I've got all the others assigned all ready, and the FBI agents are running behind. Paperwork and bureaucracy crap no doubt. For once, I wished they'd hurry up and get here so I could wash my hands of this. I don't have the strength for this, not anymore. How could I have been so wrong?"

Shock pinned Lewinsky to his chair. Disaster? Brody wanted the Feds to take over? He must have slipped into an altered universe. Maybe those chili dogs he ate for lunch were tainted. Momma warned him not to eat too much junk food, or he'd have nightmares. Course, she always said that when she was trying to get him to quit snacking and go to bed.

"Austin just called, and you're going to have to go out to Kristian's. We need someone to keep watch over Caleb. I'll send someone out to relieve you as soon as I get some back up in here."

Before Brody could completely explain the situation, Lewinsky threw up his hands in protest and blubbered,

"You want me to baby sit? All this build up and you're just sending me to keep an eye on a boy? Doesn't the brat have a nanny or something? Jeesh, how degrading is that? First, you demote me to permanent desk duty and now I have to be a...a...baby sitter!"

Utterly disgusted at Lewinsky's outburst, it took all of Brody's self restraint not to lunge over the desk at him. The imbecile might be twice his size, but he didn't have the brains of a flea. Brody made a mental note to put him in for a transfer. Maybe he could get him put on meter maid duty. At least then, he wouldn't have to share the same air with him on a daily basis.

"Stand down boy or so help me I'll knock your oversized ass so far off this force that you'll never wear a badge again. When a superior officer gives you an order, you don't belly ache about it. I believe the appropriate response would be 'yes, sir.' You launched into your little tantrum before I could give you complete information. This is not a baby sitting job. You are to guard the boy and his nanny from possible danger. Remember that man hunt you so want to be a part of? The man being hunted is Kristian's lunatic ex-husband. If he is to be believed, he already has Kristian, and it is very likely he'll eventually come after his son. You will be responsible for the boy's well being and stand guard against a possible intrusion at the home. Do I make myself clear?"

"Yeah, sure!" Lewinsky responded eagerly. Wow. Double wow. The killer was actually here in Fort Wayne. It wasn't just some wild goose chase. He was going to protect Caleb from a very real threat. Oh man, this was his big break. The one he'd been waiting for and he was going to show them all. Wouldn't it be great if this Cole person came, and he single handedly apprehended him? He could take him out with a right hook or maybe a left jab. His size made him quite the foe in the boxing ring. Yeah, buddy!!

"Is that how you address your superior? Didn't we just go over this?" Brody yelled. The boy was dumber than a box of rocks. It was like talking to a gorilla. You could tell there was life in there, but you couldn't quite get through to it.

"Sorry, sir. I would be happy to go. Err...sir, yes, sir!" Lewinsky stumbled over his response. He sat on the edge of his seat and had his leg jiggling in anticipation. The floor vibrated in time with his twitching like a miniature earthquake. Pictures danced on Brody's desk, but Lewinsky was to antsy to notice the mayhem he was causing.

"Boy, would you stop that jumping around and get on with it. You needed to be out there ten minutes ago. Get some keys from Mel, and take a squad car. Hopefully, if it looks like an officer is there, the fugitive will steer clear. Lord knows if he knew we were sending a clumsy oaf, he'd take it as an open invitation. So, you best toe the line. We've got lives at stake, and so help me if anything happens to that boy I'll choke you out myself."

Lewinsky jumped to his feet and started to salute Brody. He caught himself midway and decided he best not push it. Half skipping, half running, he headed out in search of Mel. The old guy was his ticket to a set of wheels. Man would it feel good to drive in official style for a change. After tonight, he'd graduate from rookie to full fledge cop. Maybe then they'd quite calling him "sensuous" aka "since you was" up why don't you get me something to eat. They'd have something to eat after tonight.

Before he made it out of earshot, Brody hollered,

"On second thought, take Mel with you. He can drive and try to keep you out of trouble. Maybe between his brains and your bulk you'll manage to keep things going until back up arrives."

"Damn," Lewinsky muttered under his breath. He was going to have to ride side saddle with the old fart. In the words of his nephew, dirty dirty dish rag! Oh well, at least he was finally gonna be in the middle of something instead of being the guy that heard about it the next day.

Brody watched reluctantly as Lewinsky disappeared into the other room. He half expected him to break into song. "I'm a lumberjack and I'm okay. Sleep all night and work all day." The lumbering idiot was more than he could stomach.

With no one to see him, the chief laid his head on his desk and closed his eyes. He knew he should have retired last year. Back when Chrissy talked him into staying on the force. She enjoyed the prestige of being the wife to the chief of police. Even if she didn't think he deserved the job, she liked to live off the title. Now, when he left, he would probably have blood on his hands.

Hopefully, Austin and Terrance would locate Kristian before any real damage was done. She was one of those good eggs, a rare find now a days. Most women that good looking where either self absorbed or to dumb to remember their name. She, of all people, didn't deserve this. Ugh, why is it the genuinely nice people always have the worst things happen to them? And…why did it have to happen to them on his watch? After tonight, he'd be looking for another line of work. One that involved fishing and recreational sleeping. A wave of tired washed over him, and all of his muscle creaked with exhaustion. *Just make it till the Feds show up, ole boy*, he thought. After he turned this mess over to them, he was going to blow this popsicle stand. Permanently.

Chapter 16

The bush clawed at his neck making it hard to concentrate. Cole reached back and absently smacked at one of the annoying branches. Leaves were still in the not- sure- if- I'm- ready- to- come- out stage. Not only did it make it difficult to hide, but the exposed twigs clutched at his bare skin. He had enough scratches on him to use up several boxes of Band-Aids if he were so persuaded.

Cole shifted his weight so he could rock back on his feet. His kneecaps had all the pressure they could stand. He actually heard them creak as he moved. The bushes he'd wedged himself between lined the outer perimeter of Kristian's yard. The back of the house loomed in front of him and an inside light flirted with the darkness. He hung back close to the hedges so he could use the blackness to his advantage. The weather was on his side. Not long ago, a cloud bank rolled in covering the stars. Thunder rumbled off in the distance and the breeze picked up promising rain. He wasn't much for getting wet, but maybe the impending down pour would mask any unwanted noises.

From where he sat, he could see the back of a woman's head.

A mini blind was pulled down, but the slates were still twisted open. Black bars lined her silhouette and for a moment Cole was back in his own prison. Unnerved, he chided himself on his jumpiness. He knew the cops were on his tail, but he couldn't let it affect his resolve. When he hiked in from behind, the cop car loomed in the driveway. He nearly ran back the way he'd come. It took impressive self restraint to keep his legs from turning him around. Thoughts of going back to prison plucked at his mind. One mistake and he'd be looking out from metal bars again. His time in prison made him realize just how claustrophobic he could get.

Hair piled in a bun, she leaned back on the couch watching television. The changing colors on the set reflected off the white ceiling. It reminded Cole of a kaleidoscope. Blues, reds and yellows stumbled over each other like kids scrambling for the last popsicle.

He watched for several more minutes but didn't see anyone else moving in the house. Only two rooms were lit up. The kitchen and the room with the television. Neither had any life in them other than the lady on the couch. She kept cocking her head and looking down beside her. Occasionally, he caught her lips moving. The way he figured it, his boy was probably sitting on the couch next to her. Either that or the old hag was talking to her armpit.

Seemed strange to think of him as his boy. Last time he'd seen the squall titty he was nothing but a red ball of noise. His talents were limited to screaming, sucking and filling his pants. As he lay in the dark, he tried to image what the brat looked like. No doubt, he had his momma's eyes and her holier than thou attitude. Kid probably acted like a little fairy since he didn't have any male role models other than lover boy. Snuffing him out would be doing the kid a service. He'd put him out of his misery before the other boys had a chance to knock him around. Kids on the playground could be pretty rough, especially when you pranced around like a girlie boy.

Made his skin crawl to think about any boy of his acting sissified. Kristian had set out to ruin the kid from the beginning, to make him a momma's boy. Always pampering his squalling butt and singing those stupid songs. Boy needed to be slapped around a little, just to keep him from getting soft. Heck, his ole man used to knock him around. In the long run, it made him stronger. He didn't rely on someone in a skirt to take care of him. He stood up for himself and could rough house with the best of them.

His attention jumped back to the window as he saw a little blonde head bounce into view. He stood up on the cushion beside the woman and threw his arms around her neck. Pudgy cheek pressed to hers, he gave her an exuberant squeeze. Cole spat involuntarily. What kind of boy went around hugging old ladies? Molly coddled little brats, that's who.

With his belly pressed to the ground, Cole shimmied closer to the line of darkness in the yard. He needed to get closer to the house so he could find a way to get in. From his perspective, the only ones he'd have to contend with was the old hag and the brat. Not once during his surveillance had he seen any indication that an officer was in the house. Lover boy must have left his wheels. No matter, even if he was inside, he'd be easy to take down. Especially in his worried state. Cole could just see him blubbering over Kristian. Boo hoo, the slut is missing. Boo hoo, hoo, how will I ever go on with out her. What a pansy. Besides, he couldn't be any smarter than the armed guards he'd outwitted. They'd tried to get in his way, and it cost them their lives. With any luck, he could do lover boy the same favor.

When Cole came to where the window lights illuminated the

grass, he sat up on his haunches. Once he had both feet tucked underneath him, he bolt to the corner of the house. He pulled himself up parallel to the house and waited a few moments for his heart to stop racing. About the time he decided to move, the woman on the couch stood up to head into the other room. He couldn't be sure if she noticed his approach or not.

Cole forced himself to focus all of his energy on listening. Surely, if she'd spotted him, he'd be able to hear a major commotion inside. Cocking his head to the side all he could make out was a whole lot of nothing. The television droned on, uninterrupted.

Women tended to panic, so if she'd seen him the neighborhood should know by now. Cole shifted his feet and turned to survey the side of the house that had been out of his view. A railroad tie lay on the ground hemming in some freshly planted flowers. In the semi darkness, he could just make out a window. The screen seemed loose, like the inner window was open. When the wind picked up, he could see the mesh going in and out with the ebbing breeze.

Taking care to dodge the fresh turned dirt, he edged around so he could examine the window. If the main window was open, he could pry out the screen and slide in unnoticed. The distant thunder would mask his movements.

Balanced on the wooden beam, he nearly whistled at his good fortune. Not only was the inside window open, but the screen itself sat precariously on the edge of the trim. It looked like someone had removed it and couldn't quite get it back into the original grooves. The top notches were slid in, but the bottom sat free in the window sill.

Using both hands, Cole gently forced the screen inward and pulled it completely out of its track. Turning it cockeyed, he pulled it through the window and leaned it up against the edge of the house. He placed his palms on the ledge and pushed with his legs until he could wedge his torso through the opening. The metal lip dug into his hips as he placed his hands on the floor. He nearly lost his balance, and his feet flew straight up. With as much grace as possible, he crumpled the rest of the way in the window. The carpet broke his fall and muted the thump of his ungraceful entrance.

Cole landed beside a bed with his head inches from a night stand. Any closer and he'd have a splitting headache about now. He rolled over on his stomach to try and orient himself with his surroundings. The room smelled faintly of roses, Kristian's favorite flower. As he let it envelope him, he noticed the dresser against the far wall. Drawers lay open and clothes spilled over the edges. The dim light from the hallway illuminated a lacy bra dangling from a drawer. Umm, this was definitely Kristian's room. Jewelry was strewn across the top of the dresser, like she'd been having problems deciding which necklace to wear. Wench always was a bit indecisive for his taste, Cole thought.

The room exited into a hallway. Slightly to the left, a door led into the lighted room he'd seen from the outside. He could hear the low voice of a woman and an exuberant child. The conversation sounded further away than he'd anticipated. They must have gone into the kitchen for something. It would give Cole a chance to think. He'd focused so much on getting in, he hadn't given much thought to what he should do once he got there.

Cole laid his hands flat on the carpet and rested his chin on top. The feminine smell made it hard for him to concentrate. In prison, they surrounded him with smelly men. Hairy pits and sweaty rears were a daily regiment. Nothing like close quarters with a slob to make him appreciate the simple things in life, like soap and the soft caress of a woman's perfume. He inhaled deeply and let the scent linger in his nostrils. It seeped into his lungs and rendered him temporarily immobile. The open dresser became a temptation to think about the woman who'd worn them. He mentally imaged he had personally removed each item himself. That was some lucky cotton to be up close and personal on such milky white skin.

Cole mentally kicked himself for not satisfying his thirst before he left her in the pit. It was making him crazy and distracting him from the task at hand. He got so caught up in his fantasy, he didn't realize he had company until a wet tongue slurped his face. Stifling the need to gag, he stuck his arm up to ward off anymore unwanted kisses.

A lab stood over him, tongue lolled to the side and slobber dangling from the hair on his chin. He engaged in a fully body wag, and he fixed sleepy eyes on his new find. When he didn't get the head pat he expected, the dog nuzzled Cole's neck with his cold nose.

Cole shuttered and squelched a curse. He rolled out from under the dog's leaky tongue and pushed his face with both hands. Glaring, he whispered forcefully,

"Get! You worthless mutt. Shoo."

Rather than going, the mongrel took his words as an invitation to stay. Rascal plunked down on his bottom and whipped his tail back and forth on the carpet. Swoosh,thwack, swoosh, thwack, his tail dragged across the floor and made a distinctive thump each time it hit the edge of the bed. Ears cocked in anticipation, he lowered his head so he could examine Cole with his watery brown eyes.

Cole pushed himself up on his knees and crouched over so the bed still hid his body. This mutt really rankled his nerves. Most dogs tucked tail and scadaddled for cover when he gave them his wilting stare. He had to get rid of him before he gave him away.

"Why don't you go fetch or something? Get the heck out of my face you mangy cur. I ain't got time for you're crap."

Doubling up his fist, Cole waved it for good measure. Maybe if the dog was too stupid to do what he was told, the threat of a wallop would make him mind. To his relief, the dog stood up and walked eagerly back out of the room. For an old dog, he could move with a spring in his step when motivated. Cole could hear his toenails clicking on the hardwood floor as he disappeared down the hallway.

Aggravated at the distraction, Cole try to remember what he'd been doing before he was so rudely interrupted. A slow grin teased his lips when he caught a glimpse of a pair of pantyhose. They were laying inches from his knees, just under the edge of the bed. She'd probably gotten out of them in a hurry and lost track of them in the shuffle. The thought made his blood quicken and his eyebrows narrow. If they came off in a rush, then lover boy probably had something to do with it. Anger washed over him and fueled the rage he'd been harboring since he left the cave. She'd betrayed him. Since the beginning, Kristian had been sharing her bed with dozens of lovers. To think, he'd just been daydreaming about that slut. He'd let her beauty hypnotize him again. The sensuous mouth, those voluptuous hips and his time in prison made it hard not to pant after her.

Snap out of it, he rebuked himself. Grabbing the hose, he wadded them up and tucked them in his pocket. He never did like used merchandise, so why start lusting after it now? No need to settle for an overused heel when he had virgin leather waiting for him back east.

Click, clack. This time Cole heard his visitor before he saw him. The mutt dropped a slobber soaked ball in front of him, and looked up expectantly. When Cole made no move to pick it up, Rascal nudged it with his nose and let out a bark.

The yelp echoed off the bedroom walls and shattered the silence. Cole's heart hammered in his ears, pumping adrenaline to his tense muscles. He strained to hear if someone in the other room was headed this way. Before he had a chance to brace himself, the dog started barking again. He alternated between vocals and panting. When he panted, his tongue lolled out and sent drool racing to the floor.

"Damn it!" Cole growled under his breath. That last series of barks ignited a commotion in the other part of the house. The patter of stocking feet headed in his direction. Faintly over the television a small voice hollered,

"Rascal, where are you?"

It sounded like the kid was still in the living room. Before the dog could give away his position again, Cole leaped on the dog. With his right arm tucked around the lab's neck, he gave a quick twist. In a matter of seconds, Rascal lay immobile on the floor. His windpipe crushed, he'd crumpled like a wilted piece of lettuce. Cole pulled the body behind the edge of the bed, so it couldn't be seen from the doorway.

"Rascal, come on boy, ya wanna play bad guys? I'll be the sheriff, and you can rob the bank."

Socks slapped against the carpet and whooshed as the boy slid down the wooden hallway. Small fingers grabbed the door jam to stop him from crashing into the wall beyond. Giggling slightly from the rush, he stumbled into the edge of the room.

"Rascal? Where are you? I'm looking for you and I ain't playin' no games." Caleb sing-songed into the darkness. He thumped his foot anxiously waiting for a sign that his dog was in the room.

128

Cole lay pressed to the floor with the lifeless dog pressed up against his back. Face pressed to the carpet, he could see tiny feet from underneath the bed. Jeans slumped down around his ankles, he stood on the cuff of his pants as he fidgeted.

From the other room, he heard the woman holler,

"Caleb Michael Henry, where are you at young man?" The panic in her voice was obvious. She'd lost sight of him and was frantic to make sure he was still all right.

"I'm in Momma's room looking for Rascal."

"You best leave that dog alone and get back in here, little mister." Relief turned her tone into agitation.

"Okay, I'm coming."

Cole watched the feet swivel as if to leave. They got half way turned, and then paused. To his dismay, they started walking back into the room. Crap. He rounded the end of the bed and was staring at the open window. Cole forgot to prop the screen back in the sill when he'd fallen through. It wasn't until he'd gotten halfway to the gapping hole, that Caleb noticed Rascal laying on the floor.

"Hey, Rascal, what ya doin' sleepin' in Momma's room? You're not 'posed to be in here."

He knelt down to pat the motionless dog on the head when he noticed Cole laying in the shadows. Caleb gasped and stumbled backwards. His feet tangled in his jeans, and he plopped on his bottom hard. Cole's hand flew out to cover his mouth so he wouldn't scream. With the other arm, he pulled him up against him. Caleb's arms were pinned to his side and his back pressed against Cole's chest.

Cole leaned down and whispered into Caleb's ear,

"If you wanna see your mom again, you keep that mouth of yours closed."

Caleb didn't move except for the pounding of his heart and

the slow rhythm of his lungs filling anxiously with air. His wide eyes were focused completely on Rascal. He'd never seen him that still before. Usually, even when he was sleeping his sides went in and out. Caleb gulped. Rascal's head lay at a crazy angle. The dogs ears were flipped straight up and his mouth yawned open. So many questions bubbled up inside of him, but Caleb couldn't speak. The vice grip on his face, kept him from opening his mouth.

"Caleb, what's the hold up? Am I going to have to come back there?" Gretchen yelled. She'd moved from the kitchen to the living room so she sounded even more irritated than before. That boy was going to learn to listen the first time if she had to knock it into him.

Silence greeted her last request. Strange, Caleb usually answered instantly. He might lolly-gag when he was supposed to do something, but he never avoided answering when she called. He loved to talk so much, he'd respond even if he knew he was in for a butt whoopin'. She gave him a few more seconds to answer, and then started marching towards Kristian's room.

"Boy, don't you ignore me. When I ask you to do something, I mean for you to do it NOW, not whenever you feel like it. You better hope you ain't harassing that dog again. So help me, my hand will meet that tiny heiny of yours."

As she stomped into the hallway, she half expected to see the boy come peeling out of the room or at least to get a hardy plea for mercy. Child never missed an opportunity to use his negotiating skills to try and weasel out of a paddling. The quiet began to make her uneasy. To cover her nerves, she started muttering,

"You're tap dancing on my last nerve, Caleb. Now ain't the time to be playing hide and seek, or ghost in the graveyard or whatever the heck it is you call it when you hide in the dark and try to scare people. Ooo, you better hope you have a good explanation or you're rear's going to be the bug, and I'm going to be the fly swatter."

Gretchen rounded the hallway and stood in the doorway of Kristian's room. Her chest started to ache. She didn't see any sign of Caleb. Just to be sure she decided to edge around to the other side of the bed. It would be just like the ornery little cuss to hide by the night stand. When they played hide and seek, it was his favorite spot. The space between the wall and the wooden stand fit him perfectly. If the curtains were pulled just right, no one would ever know he was there. Caleb was the only four year old she knew who had no fear of the dark and always staid silent when engaged in a hiding game. Most would yell out 'here I am' or squirm so much you couldn't miss them. This kid, on the other hand, liked to give her a heart attack. She'd start hollering for him, and he'd never say a word till she found him.

It wasn't until she was half way across the room, that she noticed the missing screen in the window. Oh my God, she thought, surely he wouldn't have gone outside without telling her. Suddenly, her whole body felt weak and a wave of pukiness washed over her. Not now, please, not now.

Gretchen stubbed her toe as she came around the far edge of the bed. She yelped from the pain and bent down to assess the damage. Her big toe felt like it should be the one saying wee, wee, wee all the way home. As soon as she had her hand pressed on her injury, she made out the hairy outline of Rascal on the floor. The darkness made everything hazy, but the dog appeared to have something wrong with him. After her earsplitting yelp, he ought to be cocking his head to see what was the matter. The old coot may be a lot of things, but deaf wasn't one of them.

Gingerly, she pushed the dog with her with her good toe. He just flopped like a rag doll. Gretchen's hand flew to her mouth, and she instinctively reached down to check his pulse. Nothing.

Not even a faint blur in his chest to indicate that he was even trying to be alive for her.

She rushed to the nightstand and tore back the curtain expecting to find a stricken little boy. If he'd discovered Rascal, he probably panicked. No wonder he hadn't answered her. He was too upset over his dog.

The hidey hole sat empty. Nothing to even show that he'd been there recently. Where would he have gone? Gretchen swallowed the lump in her throat and slowly turned back to look at the open window. Surely, even as brave as he was, he wouldn't go outside if he was upset. Ordinarily, Caleb ran to her when something was bothering him. He'd nestle into her arms and pour his heart out. When he'd lost his turtle last month, he'd cried on her shoulder until she finally convinced him that the turtle probably just went back to his mother.

With heavy feet, Gretchen trudged to the window. She didn't see anything in the yard that even slightly resembled a little boy. Looking down to think, she noticed darkened blurbs in the dirt below the window. On closer examination, she realized the fresh mud held footprints. Not the footprints of a child, but the prints of a grown man. Desperately, she tried to follow the trail with her eyes. The shadows made it too hard for her to discern which way they went.

Fighting the need to hyperventilate, she stumbled back into the kitchen. She had to get a hold of Austin before it was too late. With a low moan, she chided herself for letting him out of her sight. Why hadn't she made him sit on the bar stool while she cleaned up the supper mess? If only she hadn't turned her back, maybe he wouldn't have bolted into the other room. Where in the hello was the back up that was supposed to be here? *Dear Lord, put your arms around our boy and keep him from harm.*

Chapter 17

He slowed the car when they came to 511 North Branford. As Terrance pulled up to the curb, his front tire grazed the concrete. This was the place as best he could tell. According to the files at Kristian's office, this is where her assistant Royce lived. He didn't have a phone number listed so they had to track him down physically.

Austin flipped the door open before the car came to a complete stop and stood anxiously on the side walk waiting for Terrance to join him. His nerves were making him extra jumpy. Especially since they'd wasted so much time trying to find someone who'd seen Kristian before she disappeared. According to Terrance, if they could find out where she was headed maybe they could locate where Cole had nabbed her. Granted, it wouldn't lead them directly to her, but it would give them someplace to start investigating. If they were lucky, Cole left some indication of where he spirited her off to. *God, let them be lucky*, he begged.

Though the logic made sense, Austin couldn't hardly stomach the thought of traipsing around asking questions. He needed to be combing the countryside looking for Kristian before the monster decided he was done playing games. His chivalrous side wanted to scour the place till he found her, but the investigator in him knew it would be like finding a needle in a haystack. The hills and hollers surrounding town would take weeks to pick through, unless they had some hint at where to start. Hence, he stood here in the darkened streetlight, waiting for Royce to answer the door.

After the third slap of the old fashioned knocker, the front door swung open. Royce stood in a pair of leather slippers with a cat peeking up between his legs. His mismatched socks were pulled up to his knees and just missed the stripped boxers he had hanging to his knees. His bird legs looked extra bony since his skivvies were so large. On top, he sported an old fashioned smoker's jacket. The maroon velvet was accented with a black sash and appeared to be well worn in the elbows. Droopy jawed, he had a bowl pipe hanging between his clenched teeth. One hand held a rolled up paper and the other still hung on the door knob. His gray hair looked mussed, and the longish part he used to cover the bald spot was all askew. It stood at half mass leaving his glossy head to fend for itself.

Terrance, for once, stood speechless. He hadn't really prepared himself to be greeted by an old dude in his underwear. Somehow, he figured anybody who Kristian deemed worthy to be her personal assistant would be just a little more well groomed. Of course, the man was off the clock. But, what kind a person came to the door half dressed wearing clothes that went out of style when Sherlock Holmes disappeared. Very strange, to say the least. Maybe he should hook this weirdo up with the widow Sanders, they both look like they fell out of the same century.

Royce never said a word as he waited for them to tell him why they were there. His body blocked the entrance, and his guard cat eyed them suspiciously. He wasn't used to having visitors to share his master with. From the narrowing eyes, it was a safe bet he didn't appreciate it.

"Uhh, sorry to bother you like this Royce, but Kristian has disappeared on us and…well, I was hoping you could help us out. Do you mind if we come in?" Austin broke the silence. Out of habit, he had his hat in his hand and made the request like he was talking to a sheik. He kept his eyes lowered to show respect for the older gentleman.

Royce was the town eccentric. Back in the day, he'd been a borderline genius in the world of analytic psychology. As a professor at Kingston College, he'd enjoyed prestige and fame for his ground breaking ideas. Several years ago, he suffered a massive heart attack that gave him a permanent stuttering problem. His mind staid as sharp as ever, but he had problems expressing himself. Until Kristian came to town, he'd staid locked up in his old house. He couldn't handle the stares and awkward pity everyone showed him when he tried to talk. She was the only one who didn't judge him or make him feel uncomfortable. For that, he was eternally grateful. So, when she'd told him she needed an assistant, he'd jumped on the chance to help her out.

At the mention of Kristian's name, the older man's face melted into lines of worry. He stepped back and motioned them in. Before he could see if they were coming, he turned his back and headed into his study.

When his back turned, Terrance raised an eyebrow at Austin in question. He wasn't so sure he wanted to go inside with Mr. Crazy hair and his strange kitty. His concern heightened as he followed the narrow path to the doorway where the man disappeared. The walls had newspapers stacked against them on both sides making it impossible to do anything but shuffle through sideways.

Terrance whistled under his breath when they squeezed into the study. Bookshelves lined the walls from floor to ceiling, and they were jam packed with old books. Most of the shelves were double stacked making it seem even more impressive. At the far end of the room, Royce sat behind a large walnut desk. The top was littered with knick knacks from all over the world, including a quill pen and a miniature totem pole. On either side of it stood metal knights. The metallic life size armor had bronzed slightly, but the feathers in the helmet were as vibrant as ever. One held a large ax and the other had a spiky iron ball hanging from a chain. The hardwood floor had an oriental rug in the middle of it and a leather couch that faced the foreboding desk.

Taking Austin's lead, Terrance sat down on the edge of the couch and tried not to gawk. He'd seen a lot of things in his time, but this certainly took the cake. He kept waiting for one of those knights to start moving.

"Royce, did you catch the news this evening?" Austin queried. He hated to just jump in and start demanding information. With Royce, everything had to be slow and easy or he'd clam up on you. His stutter had him so self conscious, Austin had actually only heard him speak twice. Those times had only been because he walked in when he was having a conversation with Kristian. For some reason, when he spoke to her, he didn't worry about the fact that he stumbled over his words.

Royce shook his head. He tried to avoid the televised news and stuck to the papers. The written word somehow appeared more trustworthy since it wasn't coming from a man wearing make-up. Kind of unnerved him to see a grown man sporting lipstick, smiling into the camera and trying to shock his audience with the latest news. Seemed more like glorified gossip to him.

"Well, a man by the name of Cole Williams killed some guards on his way out of prison. His face made it on the local news because he headed this direction. To make a long story short, he's Kristian's ex-husband. We have reason to believe he already has her and plans to do her serious harm. Royce, do you happen to know where Kristian was going after she left the office this afternoon?" Austin spit out his question, and looked at the older man expectantly.

If he hadn't been watching closely, Terrance would have missed the change in Royce's eyes. They went from vacant to worried in a nanosecond. He leaned his chin on his thumbs, and his long bony fingers rested on the tip of his nose. The older man bobbled his head in assent. He narrowed his eyes in concentration, and his lips strained against his teeth.

Austin unconsciously leaned in, waiting for the response. It was almost painful to watch the man struggling to make his mouth form the words. Terrance looked from Austin to Royce and back again. As the seconds ticked passed, he wanted to yell at the man to just spit it out. But, somehow, from the way Austin waited with baited breathe, the delay was something he had expected. Jeesh, the weirdness just keeps magnifying, Terrance thought.

When the silence became tangible, Terrance snuck a peek to see if maybe the geezer had passed out or something. His head swayed with the effort, and he finally managed to say,

"J..j…j..j..j..og…g…g..g..g…ing," Royce seemed to pant with the strain. His face was red, and he kept his eyes on his desk. He couldn't bear to see the awkwardness on their faces. It was bad enough he despised himself, he didn't need the pitying looks of others to make it worse.

Austin swallowed. Okay, so she went jogging. But where at? If she'd gone out to the wildlife preserve, the trails covered over two thousand acres. They needed more information as painstaking as that was going to be.

"Do you know where she went to go running? Was it at one of the parks in town, or did she go to the wild life preserve?"

With a pleading in his eyes, Royce looked at Austin like he was asking him to run a marathon. His mannerisms said he knew the answer to the question but wasn't sure his jaws would cooperate. He frantically looked in the clutter on his desk as if he were in search of something.

Terrance watched the exchange and slowly reached into his pocket. Grabbing his memo pad and an ink pen he slid them across the table to Royce. The older man stopped fumbling around and took up the pad gratefully. He flashed Terrance a semi-smile in thanks and started scribbling on the paper. His hand shook slightly, whether it was from anxiety or a physical ailment Terrance couldn't discern.

When he finished, he pushed the pad back through the rubble to Austin. In his eagerness, Austin nearly snatched it from him before he could let go. The handwriting was rather shaky, but the note read,

> *Wilderness preserve. She said she was going to start out at the parking lot just passed the dark hollow turnoff.*
> *I think it's Buzzard's Roost.*

Austin leaped to his feet and passed the pad over to Terrance to review. He knew exactly where Royce was talking about. The graveled lot sat nestled back in some trees just off the highway. From what he could remember, the hiker's trail lead off to the east of the parking lot and wound down around the creek before it came back up towards to center of the preserve.

Now that he had a solid place to start, he itched to get back out on the highway.

Terrance stood up as well and said, "Let's ride. We should be there in less than five minutes if we play our cards right."

Before he turned to go, Austin leaned over the desk and clasped Royce's hand. When he looked up, Austin said,

"Thank you." The sob broke about mid-sentence, and he had to swallow to keep from crying.

The older gentleman squeezed Austin's hand and held him back. With an emphatic stare he stuttered,

"F..f..f..fin..d..d..d.. her..r..r..r.." The sincerity in his eyes and the strength in his hands sent a tear down Austin's cheek.

With a quick nod of his head, Austin replied,

"We will. We will."

Austin and Terrance let themselves out of the house. Royce sat in his chair, stroking his cat absently as they left. Kristian was the only friend he had left since the heart attack. She looked at the person inside the decrepit shell and loved him inspite of his frailties.

He mulled it over for a while and decided he couldn't just sit here waiting for those young men to take care of things. He knew more about where she may have headed than they did. Just last week she'd driven him out to the preserve on their lunch hour. They walked along the trail, and she showed him her favorite spot just passed the bend in the creek. Kristian liked the way the limbs hung down like a canopy. The water lapped over the rocks and made for a peaceful backdrop to think in. As frustrated as she was when she left this afternoon, he'd bet anything she headed there the minute she had her running shoes on.

Royce pushed his chair back and headed into the other room to look for his pants. He might need them if he was going to go traipsing around in the woods. Once he had them in place, he hunted down his hiking boots and a light jacket. On a whim, he grabbed his cat leash and latched it on Gargarian's collar. No reason to face the unknown totally alone. With a flashlight in his pocket, he went out the back door and jumped in his 1966 Impala. Sucker still purred like a kitten, as he backed it out of the driveway. By the time he reached the road, the young cops were completely out of sight.

Chapter 18

Terrance had his foot to the floor as they left the city limits. If everybody stayed out of his way he'd make it under five minutes. He wanted to get there, stat. With any luck, the trail would still be fresh, and they could get to Kristian before the buzzer sounded. Nothing worse than playing a game with a mad man who could change the rules or call it quits at the drop of a hat. The glow of the digital clock kept reminding Terrance they needed to hurry.

Austin sat with one hand on the dash and the other on the door's arm rest. He looked like he was ready to leap out of the vehicle at any given moment. Glaring into the darkness, he tried to make out any movement in the blackened trees. Somewhere in the dense underbrush lurked the man they were after. He just hoped they found him before Kristian paid the ultimate price. Austin couldn't help feeling responsible for her disappearance. He'd promised to protect her from the past, and yet, here she was caught in its strangle hold again. It made his stomach churn, and he silently prayed she had the strength to endure.

In a matter of minutes, their headlights hit the sign indicating Buzzard's Roost. Terrance jerked the wheel, and they squalled into the gravel pathway leading to the parking lot. As they rounded the last tree, Kristian's car sat at the far end of the graveled area.

Before Austin could jump out, his pocket started vibrating. Panicked, he fumbled to get his hand in his jeans. Desperate to answer, he nearly dropped the phone as he tried to flip it open. The display panel flashed Kristian's home, and Austin prayed everything was all right.

"Hello?" Austin answered. Terrance got stopped and headed over to inspect Kristian's car. Whatever Austin learned from the phone call could be relayed later. He decided he'd save some time and look around for himself.

When he got to the driver's door, he noticed some distinctive blobs of mud on the otherwise gray rock. The door handle had a muddy smudge right in the center of it. Sweeping his flashlight around the edge of the gravel, he noticed a fresh mound of dirt. The wind was picking up, and last year's leaves rustled through his beam of light. If he was going to locate any footprints, he'd have to do it fast. The way the sky rumbled in the distance, they were going to be in for a real gully washer. Once it hit, they'd lose any hope of picking up a trail.

Walking into the wind, Terrance followed the mud back to the mound. He needed to determine for sure if the blurbs were coming from the mound to the car or vice versa. As damp as the ground was, the misshapen prints may have actually come from walking the trail on the other side. He'd noticed that the prints wound around the trunk and headed to the trail just beyond the passenger's door.

When he reached the mound, God must have smiled on him. Right there on the side of the dirt hill was a perfect imprint of a man's boot. The toe headed towards Kristian's car, and on closer examination he could see where he'd slipped about half way down. His hand must have broken his fall, which would explain the mud on Kristian's door handle.

Eager to tell Austin his find, Terrance turned to jog back to the squad car. He nearly stumbled, when he saw his partner down on all fours. The light from the open passenger door illuminated his shaking body. From where Terrance stood, he couldn't tell if he was sobbing or vomiting. That must have been one hell of a phone call.

Terrance sprinted to Austin's side and put his hand on his shoulder. The soured smell of bile slapped him in the face when he knelt down beside him. Austin shook uncontrollably and continued to dry heave long after he had anything to get out. Between the heaving and the tears, Terrance couldn't get anything coherent out of him.

Rather than fight it, Terrance just kept his palm on Austin's back for support. No use pushing the man. Whatever he found out couldn't be good. Rushing him would only make it that much worse to get him to pull it back together. He'd seen it before with people whose loved ones were the victim of violent crimes. They'd have to break down completely before they could become strong enough to carry on. Only this time, the person being torn down was a close personal friend. So much for keeping a professional distance from the investigation, Terrance chided himself.

Austin raised up on his knees and turned so he could face Terrance. The horror in his eyes seemed even more ghastly in the shadowy light. When he spoke, his voice sounded hollow, and Terrance had to lean in to hear him.

"He has him. The heartless son of a bitch has him."

Terrance furrowed his eyebrows in confusion. He expected him to say something concerning Kristian. By the way he was heaving, he figured they were now looking for a body rather than a person.

"Has who?" Terrance questioned.

"Caleb," Austin stated flatly.

"Do what?" Terrance nearly shouted. They'd called to have back up sent out to Kristian's house over an hour ago. After they'd left, there should have been officers there within ten or fifteen minutes. Surely, he hadn't heard Austin right.

"Gretchen just called and said Caleb's gone. She'd been cleaning up the kitchen, and he went into the other room to find Rascal. When she hollered for him to come back, he'd said just a minute and never showed up. Maybe thirty seconds later, she went to see what the hold up was. She found Rascal dead in the floor and the screen window missing in Kristian's bedroom. On the ground below the window are fresh footprints big enough for a grown man."

Austin waited for his words to sink in. His heart felt like someone had recently stomped it, and he had a hard time controlling the twitch under his left eye. *Why, God, why?* he inwardly cried. Caleb was just a child. Wasn't it bad enough to turn Kristian over to the fiend without letting the bastard take her boy as well? In a matter of hours, everyone who meant anything to Austin had been taken from him. He'd waited his whole life to find a woman to share his life with and wanted nothing more than to raise Caleb as his own son. The outrage washed over him, making it impossible to think. Never before had Austin wanted so much to shake his fist at his heavenly Father. His rage built inside his chest until his lungs burned.

As his anger grew, so did the momentum of the impending storm. The winds brought the first few drops of rain and made the limbs clank together in anticipation. Face upturned, the cool water landed on Austin's face and mingled with his tears. The unexpected relief on his burning cheeks made him remember the story of Abraham. Abraham and Sarah where well into the twilight of life before they were granted the son God promised them. Isaac became the center of their world and both doted on him immensely. When the small child turned into a young man, God tested his faith. He requested Abraham to offer Isaac to Him as a sacrifice. Just before Abraham could plunge the knife in, an angel came and stopped him. God just wanted to know that Abraham's faith was more powerful than his love for Isaac.

Suddenly, an inner calm came over Austin. He couldn't explain it, but somehow his rage melted into contrition. Surely, if God could spare Isaac he could find it in his heart to help Kristian and Caleb. *Forgive me for my rage and help me channel it into the strength to find my loved ones,* Austin prayed. *May my faith be like the mustard seed that I may move the mountains to find them.*

Terrance interrupted his musings, "What in the hello happened to the back up Brody was sending? Don't tell me they got lost on the way out there."

Austin sighed, "Not exactly. They were just running behind schedule is all. Brody sent Lewinsky and Mel out since everyone else had already been assigned. They showed up when Gretchen was on the phone with me."

"Why not send Mr. Magoo and Rip Van Winkle instead? Criminey, Lewinsky can't walk across the floor without tripping over his big feet, and Mel can barely shuffle around the office with his hip the way it is."

Sarcasm dripped from every word Terrance said. He'd had a low opinion of Brody before, but now he was convinced the man was a step below anal retentive pond scum. What kind of an idiot sends officers out to stand guard if they can't even be trusted to sit on a routine stakeout? He'd made them stay in the office when he thought they were searching for a nonexistent killer. Let the man turn into a reality, and suddenly they're worthy of active duty? Man, he hoped the FBI showed up soon before Brody bungled this thing up anymore.

Austin stood completely up, and gingerly stepped around the remains of his lunch. He needed some fresh air to think. He paced to the back of the car and said,

"I had Gretchen put me on the phone with Mel. Of the two, he's the one I'd lay my money on. His body may have slowed, but he has the mind of a true investigator. He said he'd already radioed dispatch for back up. Helen told him the bureau had finally arrived. From what he understood, they were sending about fifteen agents to start searching for Caleb. By now they should be there. I told him to call back if they didn't arrive in five minutes."

He pushed a button on his cell, so the display lit up. According to his calculations, Mel would have called by now if they were still hanging. Torn between the need to search for Kristian and the desire to help find Caleb, he turned to Terrance for help. The trail on Caleb was still fresh and they may be able to catch the monster responsible. But, somehow that seemed disloyal to Kristian. Wherever she was, she still needed him.

Before Austin could vocalize his torment, Terrance had flopped into the front seat. He radioed for back up to be sent to the Buzzard's Roost parking area. Austin heard him explain that they would be searching for Kristian, and he gave a brief description of her. Before Terrance signed off, he told them he and Austin would start combing the area.

When he placed the radio receiver back in its holder, the sky finally opened up. Rain came down in a steady rush. The drops were enough to drench but not enough to make walking unbearable. Terrance headed over to Austin and quickly explained to him about the foot prints he'd found. He motioned for him to follow him down the trail headed west. The path was well defined through the underbrush even though the rain eroded any footprints they may have been able to follow. Austin knew Kristian would have stuck to the trail. Surely, the predator would have done the same. As thick as the growth was around the edges, Austin prayed they'd see a sign if someone strayed.

He was so intent watching the woods around him, he nearly smacked into the back of Terrance when he stopped. Uncertain as to the hold up, Austin walked up beside him to get a closer look. His heart sank when he saw the fork in the path.

"If you were taking an afternoon jog, which way would you go?" Terrance asked him. He had his thumbs looped in his pocket and looked perplexed. Since when did the city get creative when making a trail? Would it have been so difficult to just make one big path that wound through the whole blasted place?

Austin tried to put himself in Kristian's position, out on a carefree run through the wilderness. The trail split with one winding down towards the creek and the other went over the hill towards an open meadow. The down hill run would mean more leg work later on to get back to civilization. The path through the meadow gave a flat open space to flex the muscles without straining the lungs or the calves.

Looking from one path to the other, he finally answered,

"I'd go to the left through the meadow. Kristian likes to look at the flowers in bloom, and it'd be a less strenuous run. She jogs to relax, so I'm guessing she'd have taken the easier route."

Terrance nodded his assent, and they headed down the uphill trail. With each step, Austin couldn't help wondering if he'd made the right choice. All it would take is one wild goose chase and Kristian could be lost permanently. He swallowed hard, no pressure.

Chapter 19

He was glad the wheels he borrowed were equipped with four wheel drive. The jeep came in pretty handy when he had to maneuver through the hills behind Kristian's house. Most of the ground was uneven, and Cole had to wrestle the steering wheel to keep it straight. Each bump antagonized his bruised behind and aching head.

Cole looked in his mirror to see how his young ward was doing. Caleb sat glaring at the floor, and his lower lip pooched out in aggravation. His hands rested on his knees, and he looked like he was ready to give someone a good cussing.

For a little guy, the kid sure had a lot of spunk. He must have gotten more of his genes in him than he originally thought. It was like wrestling a double jointed mosquito trying to get him out the window and down the hill to where he'd parked the jeep. After Cole threatened to do to his mother what he'd done to Rascal if he didn't be quiet, the boy quit trying to talk. Of course, it didn't stop him from twisting his arms and flailing his legs. The turd connected with his kneecap more than once which nearly sent him tumbling into a tree. He finally remembered the pantyhose he had in his pocket and tied him up. Caleb was short enough he could string his wrists and ankles together without making him bend his back. Packing him the rest of the way was a cinch once he was immobilized.

From his calculations, they were about a mile from the back road that lead up to the cabin he'd holed up in earlier. Cole originally planned to take the boy to his mother so she could watch him breathe his last. He imagined the mortified look on her face when he plopped into her hole with her precious son in tow. She'd probably been convincing herself that lover boy would keep Caleb from harm, being a cop and all. The wench ought to know no one could stop him once he set his mind to something.

When they'd gotten back to the jeep, the sky started leaking. As eager as he was to make Kristian squirm, he wasn't in the mood to hike through a down pour with a feisty brat in tow. The cabin seemed like a more logical option. They could hole up until the storm passed. If push came to shove and it didn't let up until morning, he could improvise. Heck, he'd been doing it all night, why change gears now?

He grinned at all he'd managed to accomplish in so little time. Kristian lay at the bottom of a makeshift grave, waiting for the other foot to fall. He'd gotten into a house that was supposed to be crawling with cops and snatched his son. Even with so many things going berserk, he was still way ahead of his original plan. Cole thought he was doing pretty damn good if he did say so himself.

Before long, his headlights came to rest on his hideout, and he flipped off the engine. The cabin looked forlorn as the rain beat down, and the wind blew leaves across the porch. Nothing ever looked so good to Cole. His belly grumbled, and he had the sudden need to have some more grub. Nothing like a night stalking people to make a man hungry. With any luck, he could find some edible soup in his store and relax in the hammock. He needed to build his strength so he could finish what he started.

Caleb didn't even twitch when Cole threw him over his shoulder like a sack of potatoes. He packed him through the rain and flopped him on the floor next to the rotting couch. Fumbling in the dark, Cole found the string to turn on the only light in the room. The sixty watt bulb had so much grime on it the best it could offer was a muted glow.

With his back to the kid, Cole scrounged around in the makeshift pantry. Nothing looked good until he ran across an unopened bag of trail mix. Not much, but at least it would knock the edge off of his hunger. He headed over to the hammock and kicked back to enjoy his prize.

Before he got settled, he could feel eyes gawking at him. It was like he'd gone back to prison. He instinctively knew when the fella's in touch with their lesbian side were eyeballing him. It was the same kind of uncomfortable, only different. This time it was his kid giving him the eye, and he was pretty sure he didn't want to jump him.

Caleb sat with his knees up to his chin and looked directly at him. Even when he realized Cole was returning his stare, he didn't flinch. His eyes held a mixture of revulsion and blatant curiosity. He kept opening his mouth like he wanted to talk and then, he'd clamp his lips shut again. *Talk about creepy*, Cole thought. Those eyes seemed to look through him and probe his soul.

When he couldn't handle the awkward silence anymore, Cole finally demanded, "Speak, boy. You got something to say, spit it out." He sat on the edge of the hammock and waited for a response. Lord knows he couldn't relax until Caleb quit gawking at him.

Caleb scrunched his eyebrows together and pursed his lips

together in thought. After a few seconds, he muttered, "But…I can't."

"What the hell you mean 'you can't?' Your tongue broke or something?"

"You said if I spoke again you were going to hurt Momma like you done Rascal." Lip quivering, the boy did his best to keep the tears from rolling down his face. He jutted his chin out and wiped his nose on his sleeve.

"Forget what I said. Now, I'm saying speak. You're starting to weird me out, little man. Say what you got to say and be done with it. I can't take no more of your glaring and flappy jaw. It's dropped open and been snapped shut so much it's a wonder you haven't broken the hinge."

Caleb gulped audibly and pulled his knees up to his chest. Once he had his legs in a bear hug, he rocked back on his bottom. The scraggily couch supported his back and he blurted out, "Are you the boogie man?"

"Do what?" Cole quipped. His voice raised unnaturally as he asked the question.

"Are you the boogie man? Tyler says the boogie man sneaks in at night and tries to steal little kids when they ain't paying no attention. Whoosh, and he nabs you to sell to the bad people for extra cash, and you can't see your momma never no more. Are you going to sell me away to the bad people?" Caleb's voice cracked when he mentioned his momma. The thought of not seeing her again nearly sent the tears spilling over the self imposed dam he'd built. Even at the ripe old age of four, he was too manly to let another male see him cry.

Cole took a minute to digest what he'd just heard. The boogie man? Sell him away? He didn't know too much, but this Tyler kid must have one hellacious imagination. Either that or he just enjoyed planting ideas in little people's minds.

Around a mouth full of trail mix, Cole answered, "I ain't the damn boogie man, and I ain't gonna sell nobody. Ain't no such thing as a boogie man. Are you happy now?"

"No, not really." Honest to a fault, Caleb spit it out like it was. "How do you know the boogie man isn't real? Maybe you just haven't met him yet."

"Listen, the whole boogie man scam you got going don't make no sense. What kind a person would steal a snot nose kid that ain't worth a dime? If he's going to take the time to break in, he might as well take something that's going to bring in a little cash. Besides, the boogie man was just made up to scare little brats like you. The end."

Cole's tone said, 'that's that and now it's time to shut up.' He kicked back and assumed the problem was solved. Obviously, unaccustomed to the inquisitive ways of his son, it actually shocked him when he heard the boy say, "If you're so sure you're not the boogie man, then why did you come in and steal me 'stead of something else? You act like the boogie man. An Gretchen, she says if it acts like a duck and talks like a duck, it must be a duck. You stole a me like the boogie man so you must be the boogie man. You're just cheesn' me, so I won't be scared."

"Cheesing you? What the hell is that supposed to mean? Do you mean teasing you? Jeesh, you're like the never ending jabber jaws. Why don't you just stick a sock in it, so I can relax? Your yapper's about to get on my last ever loving nerve."

Cole let out an exasperated sigh. Lordy, and he thought the kid's mother was annoying. If he didn't cork it, he'd be forced to throttle him. He was hoping to keep him unslapped until his momma could witness the first blow. The look on her face when he connected with Caleb's tender skin, kept him going. Those green eyes pleading for mercy as his hand rose higher.

She may not beg on her own behalf, but he'd watch her squirm before the night was over.

Oblivious to the threatening undercurrent, Caleb innocently replied, "You're the one that told me to talk. I didn't say nothing until you told me to. 'Member?"

Nothing like pointing out the obvious to send someone teetering over the edge. Unable to curb his temper anymore, Cole stomped over to the boy. He cuffed Caleb's upturned face with the palm of his hand. The slap reverberated through the silence and sent Caleb's head bouncing off the dusty sofa cushion. Tears leapt to his cheeks as his teeth clamped down on his unsuspecting tongue. When he'd seen Cole raise his arm, he'd started to tell him it wasn't polite to hit. Somehow, with the blood starting in his mouth, Caleb was pretty sure the boogie man didn't care.

Stunned into silence, Caleb cradled his throbbing head in his arms. Salt water streamed down his face, and the random gulp sounded as he tried to swallow his sobs. He'd never had anyone hit him before. Least ways not like this. Gretchen smacked his bottom every now and again, but she never rattled his teeth or drew blood.

With blurry eyes, he watched his captor walk back to his spot on the hammock. Fear took over his initial curiosity, and he just wanted his momma to hold him. At home, when he had a bad dream, she'd rock him until the scariness went away. She always sang 'God is Bigger Than the Boogie Man' and told him God was always there to keep him safe.

Caleb tried singing the song in his mind to calm his quaking heart, but it just wasn't the same. A chill ran down his spine, as he thought maybe God wasn't keeping track of him no more. Maybe, when he'd said he thought his Sunday school teacher was a liar, it made God mad. Or maybe he got mad 'cause he tried to tie Rascal up. A sadness washed over him when he thought about his dog. He'd never get to play with him anymore, and they'd probably put him in the ground like they done to his hamster.

Making God mad never turned out good. In the bible, when God got real mad, he made bad things happen. Like those people who were being not nice to Noah, and he made it rain until everybody drownded. A fresh wave of fear came over him, and he silently told God how sorry he was for everything. He didn't mean to be a bad boy, sometimes it just happened.

Chapter 20

The Persian tiptoed gingerly over the wet leaves. Gargarian didn't like to be damp, let alone wet. Between the rain coming down and the puddles on the ground, he was ready to high tail it back to civilization. With a rrreow of protest, he brushed up against his master's legs to let him know his displeasure.

Ordinarily, Royce would have stopped everything to cater to his finicky cat. When he wanted his belly rubbed or another can of Fancy Feast, it was taken care of in a matter of minutes. Seeing as how he had a delicate constitution, Royce never forced him into uncomfortable situations like mingling with common cats…or walking in the rain.

Tonight was different. Kristian needed him, and that was something Gargarian would just have to understand. She'd always been there for him, and Royce wanted to be able to return the favor. Royce stooped down and ran his hand under the cat's chin. The feline arched his back and purred.

"C..c..c..c..an..t..t..t.. St..st..st..st op..p..p..p." Royce whispered into the wind. His determination wasn't lost on the spoiled cat. Gargarian looked up at him and swished his in understanding. Even though he didn't feel up to it, he guessed he could traipse around in the wetness until his master came to his senses.

Pulling his safari hat lower to block the wind, Royce continued along the trail. When they'd come to Buzzard's Roost, he saw the cop car parked cockeyed behind Kristian's. He pulled in along side the patrol car and scooped Gargarian off of his pillow. The feline rode in style on a plush, velvet covered cushion that took up most of the front seat.

As soon as he opened the door, the pungent odor of fresh vomit slapped Royce in the face. The scent came from the general area of the cop car. From the smell of it, one of the young fella's must have a weak stomach. At least Royce knew they made it this far. Hopefully, the upheaval of insides hadn't slowed them down too much.

Royce headed to the trail he'd walked earlier in the week with Kristian. He figured the cops must have had about a fifteen minute head start on him, but he still hadn't run into any sign them. At the fork in the path, he plodded confidently down towards the creek, and Gargarian pranced along disgustedly. With each step, he shook his paws in a vain attempt to rid himself of the filth.

The light from Royce's flashlight made the trees along the trail look like shadowy giants ready to pounce. Each time the wind blew, the limbs cavorted in a demonic dance. They beckoned him on like sirens leading him to a watery grave. Shuddering, Royce tried to curb his over imaginative thoughts. He had enough problems to worry about without making up phantoms of his own.

Minutes dragged as he anticipated finding the clump of trees that arched over the creek. He kept thinking it should be just around the next bend only to discover he was still clamoring through the woods. Everything looked the same in the darkness. When he'd hiked it with Kristian by his side, they'd been there before he could finish telling her about his new rose garden. She had a fondness for flowers, and he couldn't wait for her to come see what he'd done with his back yard.

Discouraged, Royce had to keep reminding himself time always went faster when she was there to ease the tension. Since the heart attack, he missed human contact and mutual conversations. Like anyone else, he craved to express his thoughts and ideas to other people. Kristian allowed him to do that without making him feel like a buffoon. Most anyone he used to communicate with had come to avoid him. They couldn't handle waiting as he struggled to speak. The awkwardness consumed all conversation, and they'd lose interest in his point before he could complete his thoughts. Kristian's patience inspired him to talk more. Regardless of what others thought, his stuttering had actually improved quite a bit with her encouragement.

Suddenly, the lapping of water on rocks carried over the sound of the wind and rain. Royce rounded a corner, and he spotted the cove he'd been looking for. The canopy of trees seemed more foreboding in the darkness, but he was certain he'd found the right place. Now, all he needed to do was see if he could find anything to indicate Kristian had made it this far in her jogging regiment.

Picturing the afternoon in his mind, he mentally saw the place bathed in sunlight. The beams touched the budding leaves and left shimmering ringlets on the ground. Doing a half turn, he faced the trail that Kristian would have come down. Slightly winded, she probably headed to her favorite boulder to catch her breath.

Royce twisted so he faced the moss covered boulder. He slowly walked the distance to the rock watching his feet as he went. His flashlight lead the way, and he tried to discern if the ground still held any tell tale footprints. This blasted rain was washing away his hopes of finding any imprinted clues to Kristian's where abouts.

Doing a slow three hundred and sixty degree turn, Royce scanned the trees in all directions. When nothing lept out at him, he plopped down on the boulder to think. How was he ever going to know if she had made it this far before the lunatic spirited her away? She'd headed to this haven, of that he was certain. He could read her like a book when she was upset. Kristian needed somewhere to reflect and pray. What better place to do that than in nature's own chapel?

Royce tipped his face back and let the cool water pelt his face. The cold drops invigorated him, and he could feel an inner calm settling over his earlier unease. He couldn't explain it, but he had a distinctive impression that she was close. *Just grant me a sign, dear Lord, so I'll know which way to go.*

Royce sat silently letting the sounds of nature surround him. Rain pattered on leaves and the wind flirted with the limbs above him. He flipped his flashlight off and waited for his eyes to adjust to the darkness. Gargarian took the opportunity to jump up in his lap. Circling three times, he plopped onto Royce's legs and nestled up against his coat.

Without even thinking, Royce began to stroke Gargarian's wet fur as he scanned the woods. Slowly, his eyes were able to make out more details in the forest beyond his little alcove. Darkened blobs became more defined, and he forced himself to focus on each shape individually. He didn't want to miss anything in his haste to locate Kristian.

In front of him, slightly to the right he could hear a steady plunk, plunk. Closing his eyes to sharpen his ears, he strained to figure out what it was. The thumping came regularly, like footsteps. Only the sound was too stuttered for it to belong to another human being. Pit, pat, pit pat of padded feet came gradually closer until it sounded like it was directly in front of him. Royce opened his eyes and leaned forward on his perch. He couldn't make out any blurbs in front of him other than the occasional shrub.

It was probably just a squirrel or a passing animal. Royce hated to turn on the light, though, just in case his assumption was incorrect. No need to spoke whatever was out there unless it was absolutely necessary. He could wait it out until it was safely out of range.

The padded steps started heading away from him and eventually grew faint enough he couldn't distinguish them from the rustling leaves. Suddenly, he heard a muted thump in the distance. The thump was followed immediately by a panicked yowl of a coyote. From where he sat, he could discern a faint struggle. As the seconds passed, the yelping grew more frantic and the flopping less controlled.

The poor animal was probably caught in a trapper's snare. Agitated, Royce decided to go see if he could help. It may not have been the sign he was asking for, but he couldn't just let the animal suffer. This was supposed to be a wilderness preserve where all wild life could flourish unmolested. Whatever hunter violated the sanctuary ought to be caught in one of his own traps. Royce didn't have much use for people who violated the laws of conservation.

Dodging brush and thorn bushes, Royce made his way towards the pitiful moan. He had his flashlight in one hand and a less than happy Persian in the other. Gragarian squirmed to where he sat tucked under Royce's arm. As they drew nearer to the mournful animal, he commenced to growling low in his throat.

When they finally broke through the underbrush, Royce could just make out the shadowy form of mangey coyote. He edged in until he could illuminate the animal in his beam. As soon as the light hit him, the coyote laid his ears back and bared his teeth. He struggled to pull his leg up off the ground, but couldn't get it to budge. His hind leg was stuck into the dirt up to his knee joint.

Royce couldn't believe what he was seeing. No metal trap or string lay anywhere near the coyote. His leg looked to be pinned in a hole. Inching closer, he laid Gragarian down so he could kneel down on the ground. He wanted to get a better look at what he was seeing. The cat went berserk and clumsily climbed up on Royce's back. Fortunately, his claws weren't long enough to penetrate his jacket.

From the new vantage point, it looked like some sort of wooden slat pressed the coyote's leg next to the dirt lip. The top of the board was littered with leaves and twigs, but the animals flailing had scattered most of them. Each time the coyote jerked to free his leg, the board scraped against his fur. A dark red spot was beginning to form around the area nearest the wooden slat, and his efforts were gradually wearing him out.

Royce looked around him to see if he could find anything to try and knock the coyote free. As much as he hated to see him suffer, he didn't want to put himself in harms way trying to get him loose. Gragarian was too cute to become coyote fodder, and he had better things to do than nurse a bite wound.

Fumbling around, he finally ran across a limb that might be big enough to reach the board without putting him in too close to those angery teeth. Royce wrestled it off the ground and shimmied the end of it towards the trapped animal. He sure hoped the coyote would run away rather than attacking. Supposedly, coyotes didn't usually bother with humans since they were more afraid of people than people were of them.

When he had the end of the limb pressed against the offending board, he tried to weasel it underneath to use as a lever. Once he had it slightly under the edge, he pushed down forcing the plank to pop up for a brief second. That was all it took for the coyote to pull free. He jerked his leg out and eyed Royce warily before he scampered off into the woods.

As soon as the coyote was out of sight, Gragarian scampered down a tree and plastered himself to Royce's side. Out of morbid curiosity, Royce went over to examine the unwitting trap. Up close, he was able to confirm his belief that it was a wooden plank that had to have been placed there by somebody. The plywood seemed out of place amidst all of the leaves and dirt. Who would go to all that trouble, and what exactly were they covering up? Gragarian meowed half heartedly at his side while Royce knelt down to inspect. He gripped the edge and managed to move it just enough to see a gaping hole.

Chapter 21

The darkness had gotten thicker after her visitor left, and she struggled to get her lungs to fill with air. An incubus of fear settled on Kristian's chest slowly sucking her breath away. Her weary body ached from the abuse she'd taken today, and she just wanted to slip into unconciousness. Muscles begged for sleep, but her worried mind kept her flirting with consciousness.

She'd known fear before, but this was different somehow. This completely consumed her senses leaving her too exhausted to remember any Bible verses. Those verses were her defense against insanity, and she'd lost them. In the midst of her maternal panic, she'd forgotten all of the reassuring words she'd committed to memory. The helplessness as she waited and worried only magnified the reality that she wasn't going to be there to shield Caleb from this monster. The monster she had provoked.

Kristian kept seeing Caleb's face contorted in fear. That was the one emotion she'd swore he'd never have to know. Especially at the hands of his father. Up to this point, she'd protected him from any real scariness. In fact, he was probably the only four year old in Fort Wayne who would plunge into a darkened room without hesitation. Caleb had an inner confidence and innocence that didn't allow for any misgivings. He greeted each new day believing everything was going to be all right. Now, in the matter of one night, his entire world would be turned upside down. She just hoped the worst thing to be shattered was his innocence. Kristian didn't think she could go on if she lost her son.

Head bowed, she strained to pray, but she couldn't form the words. In her heart, she felt God knew what she needed. She just needed it to be His will to carry it out. As she sat there struggling in the void, the faint sound of footsteps interrupted her thoughts. Her heart picked up speed, and she clenched her aching jaw. How much more of this was she going to be expected to take?

Suddenly, she heard the muted sound of something soft scraping against the top of the cave. It was followed by a blood curdling scream. The unexpected sound tore through Kristian like a bullet. Her stomach bottomed out, and she felt the blood draining from her head. For a moment, she struggled with self imposed blackness, before she was able to come to her senses. When the sound came again, she could register it belonged to an animal and wasn't the screams of her own son.

Cole must not have gotten the lid put back in place when he left. Staring up into the darkness, she could make out the faint outline of something dangling into the cave. The black was still all consuming where she lay, but it had a grayer quality up towards the surface where the board had been moved. In between yelps, she thought she heard another set of footsteps.

Kristian stared intently at the opening, and suddenly the lid popped up. The coyote pulled his foot out, and the lid flopped back down at a funny angle. She heard the wounded animal yelping off into the distance. With it gone, she was certain that someone or something else was still up there. Dull thuds echoed through the ground and came to a stop just above where she lay.

The yellow beam of a flashlight glowed faintly above as it was plunked to the ground. It illuminated a set of fingers that gripped onto the edge of the wooden plank. With a grunt, the top was removed, and Kristian saw the back of a man's legs. Expecting the worst, she instinctively started saying the Lord's prayer. *Our Father, who art in Heaven, hallowed be thy name. Thy kingdom come, Thy will be done…*

Kristian was unable to finish. As soon as she got to the 'thy will,' the full beam of the flashlight slapped her in the face. Completely blinded, all she made out was a glowing yellow orb and a darkened silhouette. Unable to raise her arms, she squinted against the brightness and tried to orient herself. A movement beside the man's leg, caught her attention. Kristian shook her head in disbelief. A white Persian cat wound himself in and out of his legs. The fluffy tail laced around the pant legs with affection. She only seen one cat like that before. But, why would Gargarian be out here in the middle of nowhere. Her heart leapt when she heard, "K..k..k..krist..t..t..ian!"

"Royce, is that you?" Kristian croaked. Her throat had gotten dry, and her face felt swollen. She didn't realize how much damage had been done to her mouth, until her lip split. The sting sent blood to the surface and a tear to her eye.

He turned the flashlight towards himself and nodded his assent. Relief flooded over her, and she silently thanked God for sending her a second savior. She couldn't imagine why Royce would be out here on a night like this, but she was eternally grateful that he was.

"Y..y..y..y..you ok..k..k..kay?" From where he stood, she

looked like she'd tangled with a grizzly and lost. Her leg twisted into a crazy angle, and he couldn't really tell if her arms were still functioning. The puddle of dried blood near her head and her misshapen face broke his heart. Her ex must have been some kind of animal to do this to her. Royce had the overwhelming desire to hunt the man down and choke him out himself.

"Yeah, I'm going to be, now." Kristian swallowed and licked her aching lips. "You have to send help for Caleb before it's too late." Now that she had someone who could do the leg work, she desperately wanted to get her son out of danger. Cole would be plotting to take him the next chance he got, and she wanted to have him well hidden before he did.

Royce wasn't sure he'd heard her right. The blow to her head must have done more internal damage than he originally thought. Here she lay contorted at the bottom of an underground cave, and she wanted someone to help her son. If he knew Gretchen, the boy was probably well fed and tucked into bed by now. The woman wasn't making any sense.

He started fumbling in his pocket and pulled out a book of matches. Kristian watched in disbelief. She needed him to get the police to save Caleb, and the man wanted to smoke his pipe. He had a quirky habit of packing his pipe and enjoying the smoke when he had something he wanted to mull over. Ordinarily, she found it quaint, but tonight it became a source of irritation.

"Royce, you don't have time to light your pipe now. You have to get a hold of Austin and have the police send protection for Caleb. The man who did this to me is after Caleb. We have to warn the cops so they can keep him safe. Forget about me, just make sure my son doesn't disappear."

To Kristian's dismay, Royce continued to pat down his

pockets like he hadn't even heard her. A satisfied smile came to his lips when his hand came into contact with something in his pocket. He held up a finger on the hand with the flashlight, as if telling her to hold on a second. Before she could protest, he stepped back out of sight. Gargarian stayed at the lip and peered down at her curiously.

Great, Kristian thought, the cat was interested but Royce'd gone to smoke. He usually savored his pipe for ten or fifteen minutes before he was ready to discuss anything. Every second wasted gave Cole another second to close in on Caleb, if he hadn't already nabbed him. That was a possibility she wasn't ready to entertain just yet.

Up above, Kristian heard a sizzle and the acrid smell of gun powder wafted down to her. Just as she registered the scent, a high pitched whistle sang out followed by an explosion. The trees above were illuminated momentarily in a bluish white light. Gargarian nearly stumbled into the hole with her when he jumped. His hind feet skid over the edge, but he managed to claw his way back to safety with his front paws. The angry screech he let out reverberated even after the bang had subsided.

Satisfied the young cops had heard his bottle rocket, Royce went back to keep watch over Kristian. He plopped down on his bottom and sat Indian style on the edge of the cave. He positioned himself so he could keep an eye on Kristian. Gargarian jumped into his lap huffily and flicked his tail in Royce's face.

Royce reached down and patted the cat's head in apology. Poor thing had been through a lot tonight, but he was just going to have to endure a little bit more. He wasn't going to leave his ward until help got there. With one hand tucked around the cat, he used the other to stroke his matted fur. Gargarian raised his back legs in appreciation and graced Royce with a rumbling purr.

Exasperated, Kristian raised her voice irritably, "Royce, don't you understand? Caleb is going to be kidnapped or possibly killed. You have to go inform the police so they can protect him. Now!"

Her injuries were making her irritable, Royce thought. He'd never heard her raise her voice before, much less bark an order. What she needed was some medical attention. The pain was making her talk out of her head. Caleb wasn't in any immediate danger, not with Gretchen on duty. No one could get past her nanny, even if they were armed to the teeth. Old hard nose would send him packing with a knot on his head. Besides, he wasn't about to leave her out here all alone. What if her ex came back? He'd do her in before anyone was the wiser. Royce wouldn't let that happen, even if she was cranky.

Royce leaned over so Kristian could see his face, "I'm st.st..st..staying."

"Please, Royce, you have to help Caleb. I'm not going anywhere, just send someone back for me after you make sure he's safe. I'm begging you." The pleading in her voice made Royce shift uncomfortably. It may be the injuries talking, but she was sincere in her concern for Caleb. As much as he wanted to please her, he couldn't justify leaving her alone. If he left and something else happened to her, he'd never be able to forgive himself.

"N..n..n..no. N..n..n..not un..ntil Aust..st..st..in g..g..ets here." His decision was final and his tone didn't leave any room for argument. He flipped his flashlight off to preserve the battery and settled in to wait.

Defeated, Kristian decided she'd better save her energy rather than waste it arguing with Royce. The man was an obstinate old cuss when he wanted to be. If Austin was coming, he'd help her keep Caleb safely out of Cole's way. Butterflies danced in her belly as she fought to keep her composure. The pain she felt now would be nothing compared to having Caleb harmed. *God, let Austin hurry.*

Chapter 22

Terrance snapped to a stand still, and Austin ran into the back of him. The crack sounded like gunshot coming from the west of them. Both turned in time to see a burst of white light just above the tree line. It appeared to be not more than a couple of miles from where they stood in the field. If Austin remembered correctly, on old creek ran through pretty close to there.

Not long before, a coyote yelping had come from the same direction. Lead settled in Austin's belly when the first yowl rang out. It sounded like someone screaming in pain. He stopped dead in his tracks and waited until it rang out again. Terrance muttered, "Coyote, no doubt."

After a few minutes for Austin to regain his composure, they'd continued on in their search. So far, they hadn't seen anything to indicate Kristian had come through here. The farther they went, the more Austin questioned his decision to come this way. Maybe she'd gone past the creek instead of through the field. If that were the case, they'd just wasted thirty minutes going in the wrong direction. He'd just about talked himself into asking Terrance to turn around when the fire cracker went off.

"Who shoots fireworks in the woods on a rainy night?"

Terrance asked. Seeing the bottle cap explode seemed as out of place as a hound dog in a crystal laced ball room. It was still a few months before the fireworks stands opened in Fort Wayne.

Austin scratched his head and shrugged. "Someone who wants to be noticed?"

"Exactly. Let's say we go check it out. Not like we're doing much good out here."

Austin nodded his ascent and fell in step behind Terrance. Rather than back tracking down the trail, they headed out in a straight shot towards the noise. Their progress slowed as they wrestled with the brush and sticker bushes. Each time a thorn bush tore at his clothes, Austin couldn't help thinking of Caleb. He'd taken the boy for a walk through the woods behind Kristian's house last Saturday morning. Caleb stood just high enough that the undergrowth hit him in the face. He'd bound off threw the thornless bushes and let them slap him with out a care in the world. The occasional briar patch mingled in with the harmless weeds, and he'd get all tangled up. At one point, after a particularly thorny bush drew blood, Caleb turned and hollered for Austin to "watch out for the horns."

Austin brushed a tear from his cheek and tried to be more careful of the "horns." He hoped the search faired well for Caleb. If the FBI took over, they might stand a chance of locating him before Cole got too far. With the rain and his unfamiliarity with the area, it might slow him down enough to give them the opportunity to catch up.

When Terrance came up on a log, he stopped with one foot resting on the rotting bark. They'd been walking for over ten minutes and still hadn't found anything. He wanted to double check with Austin to see if they'd veered off course.

"Where would you say that bottle rocket came from?" Terrance asked.

Austin visualized it in his minds eye again and tried to judge the direction. The rain and darkness made it hard to be certain they were going the right way. From what he remembered, the source ought to be relatively close to the creek that runs through the middle of the wilderness preserve. If they could stumble onto the creek bed, they could follow it until they ran across something.

"I'd say it has to be pretty close. There should be a creek that runs down through here somewhere. The blast came from where the trees dipped lower on the horizon. If we could find the creek bed, we'd at least be in line with where the light started."

Terrance nodded. "This creek have any water rolling in it?"

"Ought to," Austin replied. "After our downpour last week, it out to be running good."

Terrance cocked his head to the side and listened. He turned his flashlight off so he could concentrate. The wind rustled the tree limbs, and water droplets pattered on the half open leaves. Without the crunching of their boots on the leaves, he thought he could hear a faint gurgling in front of him. He tapped Austin on the shoulder and pointed. Austin bobbed his head in assent. He could hear it, too.

The two plunged off towards the sound. They got to the top of the next ridge and an eerie orange glow came into view. About three feet off the ground, the orange blob shimmered and would randomly glow brighter. Austin reached up and grabbed Terrance's arm. Pulling him behind a big tree, he had him turn off his flashlight.

"Did you see that?"

"See what?" Terrance questioned. He'd been staring at the ground trying to keep from tripping over the rocks littering the hillside. Only thing he'd seen were some rotten leaves and an occasional twig.

"About a hundred yards dead ahead there's something glowing."

Terrance poked his head out and looked. Sure enough, an orange glow floated in the darkness ahead. Tilting his head to the side, he concentrated on the spot. The damp wind picked up, and he got a waft of tobacco smoke.

"I'd say someone's smoking, probably a pipe," Terrance whispered to Austin. Judging the height, whoever it was must be sitting on the ground.

"What do you think about splitting up? You stay here, and I'll circle around behind. Once I get around, I'll try to surprise him from the rear. You can cover me."

Austin leaned in towards Terrance as he awaited his response. His adrenaline started pumping and it echoed inside his ears. Who ever it was couldn't be up to anything good sitting in the middle of the woods smoking in a rainstorm. The hairs on the back of his neck stood at attention, and his nerves tingled. This might actually be the one they were searching for. Once he got his hands on Cole, he'd squeeze his windpipe until he told him where Kristian was. If he'd done anything to her, the bastard would answer to him...and his twenty five millimeter. Nothing would make him feel better than to watch him eat lead and die.

Sensing the tension in Austin, Terrance hesitated to respond. The man was just too close to the situation personally to be trusted sneaking up behind anybody. With his volatile temper, he was liable to draw blood first and ask questions later. If the glowing pipe had Cole attached to the other end, Austin could very well snap. The last thing he needed was to start a full scale shoot out in woods that could start crawling with FBI agents at any given time. In fact, he was relatively surprised they hadn't shone up already, flashlights blazing. So far, the only other human they'd encountered had been whoever sat down there enjoying his smoke.

"We can separate on one condition. We both go around behind. You hang back and cover me while I try to sneak in for a closer look. By cover me, I mean keep you're gun in your holster until I signal for help."

"What kind of jerry-rigged condition is that? How am I supposed to help you if I keep my gun sheathed until you signal? Cole is a cold blood killer. You could be dead before I managed to raise a weapon."

Austin's frustration dripped from every word. Terrance wasn't making any sense. He knew what they may be up against. Heck, he'd even seen the pictures of the mutilated guards. Cole meant business, and Austin didn't intend for him to harm anyone else tonight.

Terrance put his hand on Austin's shoulder and pressed firmly. Austin started to shrug away, but stopped himself in time. Terrance meant business, and his grip suggested he'd be willing to come to blows if the occasion arose. Deep down, Austin knew his friend was only trying to protect him from himself. As much as he hated to admit it, his anger could very well be his undoing tonight. Swallowing hard, he forced himself to calm down long enough to entertain what Terrance had to say.

"Listen, I know you're angery, but we don't even know for sure if Cole is attached to the other end of that pipe. You go down there half cocked, and somebody's liable to get hurt. I just want you to hang back until I can identify our target. Even if it is the bastard we're after, we won't accomplish anything if we kill him. He's our only connection to Kristian."

Reluctantly, Austin had to admit Terrance was right. He mentally kicked himself for being so rash. In a matter of hours, his entire approach to life had been completely twisted inside out. If someone would have told him over his bowl of Fruit Loops this morning that he'd be lusting for blood before bedtime, he'd have scoffed at him. Austin had never known such rage towards another person or anything really. His anxiety over Kristian and Caleb definitely clouded his judgment.

Bowing his head, Austin said, "I'm sorry. You're right. I'm just stressing. We'll do whatever you think is best. Just give the word."

Terrance patted his back in understanding and motioned for him to follow him. He circled back and headed around to the left of the pipe smoker. Whoever it was appeared to be sitting at an angle, and Terrance wanted to be sure to stay far enough in the shadows they wouldn't be detected. Slowly, they tiptoed over the damp leaves using the wind and rain as a cover for any swishing their wet clothes made.

Finally, they stood directly behind the man. Terrance held his palm out and motioned for Austin to stop. Once they were both immobile, he continued on alone. When he got within ten feet, his foot came down on a twig. The snap coordinated with a dead spot in the wind, and seemed to magnify in the darkness. Cursing his bad luck, Terrance held still hoping the man hadn't heard him. He stood completely exposed. All the trees around him were no bigger around than a flag pole. With his sturdy frame, he'd never be able to blend into the scenery.

Just when he thought he could breath easy, the man whirled and hit him dead in the face with a flashlight beam. The light temporarily blinded him, and he couldn't see who wielded the other end. Terrance held both hands out to his sides. Far enough to show he didn't have a concealed weapon but close enough he could still reach his holster in a pinch.

He heard Austin slide his pistol out of its holster, and the man must have heard it too. Instantly, the light was taken out of his face, and the man held it up under his chin. The beam illuminated his face, and his full toothed grin nearly made Austin drop his gun.

"Royce, what in creation are you doing out here? I nearly put a bullet between your eyes!" Austin bellowed. The adrenaline still pounded in his ears and made his hands shake. He'd already taken his safety off and had a finger on the trigger. His stomach rolled over as he realized just how close he'd come to drilling a hole in Royce.

Royce shrugged his shoulders. He motioned towards a hole behind him with his flashlight. It gaped open about three feet from where he'd been sitting and a piece of plywood lay haphazardly to the side. Slowly, Royce moved the beam of light from the officers back to the hole. When neither seemed inclined to come look, he cleared his throat and stuttered, "K..k..k..krist..t..t..ian."

His matter of fact tone made it clear he was making a statement and wasn't merely inquiring about their investigation. Terrance raised an eyebrow quizzically. This guy was even weirder standing in the woods with his pants on, than he was in his skivvies back at the house. For some reason, he couldn't bring himself to believe he'd heard him correctly.

Just as Terrance noticed the Persian winding around Royce's legs, Austin bolted passed him and snatched the flashlight from Royce. Dropping to his knees next to the opening, Austin shined the light down into what appeared to be an underground cave. It took a moment for his eyes to adjust. When they came into focus on the mangled mess at the bottom, he choked, "Oh my God!"

The sob hung in his throat as he took in the horror. Kristian's head lay in a dark pool of blood, and her face was grossly distorted. Lips swollen and bloody, he wouldn't have recognized her except for the hair. Slowly he allowed his eyes to rove from her head down the full extent of her body. Her arms lay limp on her stomach and one leg twisted into a crazy angle.

Frantic, Austin stared at the spandex top, willing it to move up and down. He needed some indication she hadn't already left him. Flopping down flat on his belly, he leaned in to where his upper body hung down into the cavern. Arms out stretched, he tried to get the light as close as possible.

Terrance instinctively came over and latched onto Austin's ankles. The man looked like he was going to do a swan dive into a cavernous void. He motioned Royce over to hold Austin into place, and he went over to see what had him so rattled.

He instantly flinched when he saw her body. Even though the shadows made it hard to tell, Terrance felt like they were dealing with a homicide rather than a search and rescue. Between the pool of blood and misshapen limb, it seemed all to familiar. How many times had he drawn the chalk line around bodies that had the same tell tale signs of foul play? Swallowing his disgust, he reached down and put an arm on Austin's shoulder. To think, the same bastard who'd done this now had Caleb. Terrance hoped they'd find him before he ended up in the same predicament.

Unwilling to believe, Austin continued to stare at the lifeless form and pleaded for God to make her breathe. When he still couldn't make out any movement in her chest, he locked in on her puffy eyelids. With all his might, he willed her to open them. He didn't have the strength to carry on if Kristian went out on him now. *Please, God, I need her,* he prayed.

Suddenly, her eyes fluttered open, and Austin nearly

dropped his flashlight. Joy and relief flooded over him, and his tears finally came full throttle. The salt water mingled with the rain on his face making it hard to keep Kristian's face in focus. His heart danced, and he couldn't helping thinking this must be how Lazarus's family felt when Jesus called him from the grave.

His merriment stumbled mid-stride when he heard her say, "Where's Caleb?"

Austin's smile froze, and his eyes widened. How was he going to answer that? He couldn't lie to her, but he didn't want to worry her so much she made herself worse, either. The silence grew louder as he debated what to say. Unfortunately, his quiet said more to her than any words could.

"You have to get him back."

The command hung heavy between them and the ball in Austin's stomach found its way back. He knew in his heart more than just Caleb's life hung in the balance. If he couldn't come through, the Kristian he loved would stay in this pit...forever.

Bless those searching for the boy, Austin prayed. His mouth had gone suddenly dry. It felt like an army of cotton swabs took up residence on his tongue.

Chapter 23

Wringing her apron with her hands, she dipped her head between her knees. Gretchen wheezed to get some air as she hyperventilated for the third time tonight. She was beginning to think she'd turned into some kind of pansy or something. Next thing you knew, she'd be asking Mammy to bring her some smelling salts. Disgusted, she succumbed to her aching lungs and hee, hee, whoed until she could feel the pressure easing.

The air finally started coming in manageable doses, but Gretchen kept her head down to think. She lay her forehead across her arms and let the nights events role over her like an old fashioned movie projector. Ever since Austin burst in here spouting off about Cole, her house had turned into a scene from one of those low rated police videos. When Austin said officers would be coming to keep an eye on them, she'd assumed the only person she needed to worry about was Kristian. The back up she'd been waiting for turned out to be Barney Fife and his faithful sidekick, Gommer Pile. They'd gotten into an argument over who got to drive and wound up being ten minutes too late.

Lordy, if those jokers were the only thing that stood between

Caleb and harm, they might as well throw in the towel now. Gretchen kicked herself again for not chaining the boy to her side the minute Austin left. The little turkey never could hold still and now…well…now, she just hoped he'd still be able to squirm when they found him. A wave of nausea replaced her previous oxygen problem.

Raising her head, she put her hand to her lips and forced her stomach back into its rightful place. As she struggled to regain her composure, Gretchen met eyes with the oversized oaf who was supposed to be an officer from the local force. If he wasn't putting his foot down in the wrong place and stumbling, he was choking on it as he continually put it in his mouth. When the federal agents finally showed up, she was never so happy to see someone in all her born days. Men dressed in all black never looked so good.

The goober just kept gawking at her from across the room, and Gretchen couldn't take it anymore. By golly, if he wanted to stand around taking pleasure in her discomfort, she'd just give him something to be uncomfortable about. Wagging her finger for emphasis, she said, "Boy, you best find something else to look at before I come over there and knock those eyeballs plum out yer knobby head."

Lewinsky blushed and bumbled to avert his eyes. He wasn't trying to stare, but he'd never seen Gretchen show any sign of weakness. Since he'd been here, she'd done nothing but wheeze and fight back tears. It was like watching the terminator cry over a sappy movie. No matter how you looked at it, it was all kinds of strange. He didn't know whether to offer her a kleenex or tell her to suck it up.

Gretchen's eyes bore a hole in the back of his skull as he turned to walk away. Ever since the FBI agents took over, he and Mel had been told to stay in the kitchen out of the way. Just to make sure they followed orders, two rather crusty individuals were staked out at the doorway to make sure they stayed put. Ever since they were taken out of the action, Mel leaned against the wall. His eyes pointed out the window, but the vacant look suggested he was deep in thought.

Not as gracious as Mel, Lewinsky flopped down in a kitchen chair and audibly proclaimed the injustice of making him sit at the table like some kid in time out. Between firing the guard dogs dirty looks and gawking at Gretchen, the oaf pretty much wore out his welcome.

Several federal officers were back dusting for finger prints in Kristian's room and the rest were trying to follow the trail he'd left on the way out. Seemed pretty asinine to him. Why waste your time dusting for prints when you already knew who the suspect was? Wasn't like the swirls on his thumb were going to mystically tell them where he'd spirited the kid off to. It didn't take anything more than common sense to know that. But, oh no, since he didn't have on a fancy pants suit or go through all that FBI training, his thoughts were considered unintelligent.

Lewinsky sauntered past the agents on guard and peered into the living room beyond. The pair fired him a drop dead look, so he flashed them his best debonair smile. They stepped closer together and tried to stretch out to block his view. No matter how much they maneuvered, they were still a head shorter than Lewinsky. He cockily thumbed his nose at them and took in as much of the scenery as he cared to. He couldn't really see any of the action, but it made him feel better to tower over the Feds. Much like a belligerent child, he had to show he could do what he wanted, when he wanted and ain't nobody gonna stop him.

After he'd had his fill annoying them, he turned to go talk to Mel. As he was walking away, he heard a walkie talkie buzz on in the other room. Straining to hear, he stopped in his tracks and leaned not so subtly towards the sound. The static blurbed in and out between words, but it sounded like the boys on the outside found tire tracks back in the field behind the house. They "belonged to a jeep" and the driver "appeared to be in quite a hurry." He couldn't be sure, but he thought he heard them say he'd "flung mud everywhere."

The transmission ended almost as quick as it began, and Lewinsky mulled the information over in his mind. Suddenly, his eyelids flew up as his brain made the connection. On his way back to town tonight, he'd seen muddy tracks coming from the outskirts of the wildlife preserve. He snapped his fingers and muttered, "That's it!"

Everyone turned to give him a stick-a-sock-in-it look. Gretchen looked like she was actually reaching for her rolling pin. However, Lewinsky was oblivious to it all. Half skipping, half hopping, he lumbered over to Mel. He wanted to fill him in on his little tidbit of information. Being old, he was probably familiar with the area and could help him figure out what the fugitive would be doing out that direction.

Lewinsky nearly didn't get his brakes on in time, and stumbled when he closed in on Mel. Fortunately, the older man still had good reflexes and managed to dodge a flailing arm. It crashed into the wall just behind him, and he just shook his head at the younger man's clumsiness. Man was he glad Brody didn't send him out with this bumbling idiot more often. Mel had been happy to get a chance to flirt with the action, but if it meant having to baby-sit baby Huey, he'd have just as soon staid back at the station.

Mel waited with raised eyebrow as Lewinsky collected his thoughts. The near fall seemed to have knocked the words right out of him. It was almost painful watching the wheels turn as he tried to remember what he wanted to say. Mel hoped he'd spit it out soon because he looked like he was going to rupture something, or maybe it was a bad case of gas. Either way, Mel didn't want to be standing to close when he released the pressure.

Lewinsky glanced over at the FBI agents and waited until they'd found something better to focus on. He didn't want them overhearing his conversation with Mel. Knowing his luck, they'd try to take credit for his discovery, and he'd still be stuck holding down a kitchen chair. He didn't come all this way to miss out on the action. He'd waited for this opportunity too long.

When he was certain no one else was paying attention, he whispered to Mel, "Did you hear that?"

"Hear what?" he asked out loud. Mel scratched his head and looked at Lewinsky like he'd lost his mind. Only thing he'd heard recently was his stomach growling. The lingering smell of spaghetti in the kitchen reminded him he hadn't eaten any supper.

Lewinsky reacted like he'd poked him in the butt with a hot iron. He pursed his mouth, stuck his finger to his lips and blew. Nodding his head towards the agents, he expelled air like his insides had sprung a leak. The bubble in his head holding all the hot air must have finally busted loose, Mel thought.

"Quiet!" Lewinsky whispered emphatically. "We don't want them to hear us."

"Oh, we don't?" Sarcasm dripped from Mel's words.

"No. This is just between us. You and me and no one else until the time is right. Agreed?"

Lordy, Mel thought, how'd he get to be so lucky all in one day. Mr. Clumsy wanted to take him into his confidences and share his secret with him. There was a woman not ten feet away, and he wants to confide in him. He just hoped it wasn't about "touching." Last thing he needed was to hear a boat load of touchy, feely crap from this goober.

Taking his silence as consent, Lewinsky continued, "I just heard them say they found muddy tire tracks back behind the house. It got me thinking, on my way back into town, I saw muddy tracks coming out of the wildlife preserve over by widow Sanders. They fanned out from the ditch, and I remember thinking they seemed totally out of place. I bet it's him."

Mel raised an eyebrow and waited to see if Lewinsky was going to give him any more details. After all that "secret" stuff, he was expecting something a little more juicy. Just because he saw muddy tire prints, and they found muddy tire prints behind the house didn't mean they were made by the same vehicle. It was only raining out side and anyone who went off roading would be leaving tracks, but...who was Mel to say?

In spite of his desire to shred Lewinsky's scatter brained theory, he couldn't help thinking maybe he was onto something. In all of his years investigating, it never failed. The hair brained schemes were usually the ones that brought them the closest to capturing the bad guy. Swallowing his sarcasm, Mel asked, "Where exactly were the tracks? Was it inside the confines of the preserve?"

Lewinsky thought about it and tried to bring up a mental image of where he was when he saw them. He'd originally thought it was inside the preserve, but now that he thought about it, he wasn't so sure.

"Come to think of it, I'm pretty sure it was to the outside of where the preserve starts. I'd say it was probably a mile or so from the first parking lot. Why's that?"

If those tracks did belong to the fugitive they were looking for, what would he be doing out that far from town? Mel ran over the area in his mind. The preserve itself wouldn't offer too much as far as protection. It was nothing but woods and wide open spaces. With all the rain they got tonight, he'd almost bet Cole would want to find somewhere out of the way and dry to hole up.

On the outer edge, pretty near to where he thought Lewinsky was talking about, some boys from Sioux Falls had a cabin. Place stayed desert most of the year, but they always kept it stocked full of supplies just in case. They never knew when they might get the urge to go hunting, and they didn't want to have to stop by a supermarket first. He'd been out there a few times to help show them around the area.

The more he thought about it, the more he convinced himself the cabin would be the perfect place for a kidnapper to take his prey. It was out of the way, and no one ever went out there. In fact, probably only a handful of people knew it even existed.

Clearing his throat, Mel made eye contact with Lewinsky and stated flatly, "Somewhere around in there is a cabin. The old access road has grown over with weeds and grass, but it comes out on the highway right where you were talking about."

Lewinsky felt his blood moving faster as his heart picked up the pace. So, he wasn't just imagining things. He truly could have information that would lead them right to the fugitive. He licked his lips anxiously and quipped, "Wanna go check it out?"

"We need to let the agents know. They're more equipped to handle the situation if it turns out to be more than a dead end. From what I've seen, that boy doesn't stand a chance if we go out there alone to try and save him. You saw the pictures of those guards, and they were actually trained to handle killers."

Lewinsky heard the words coming out of Mel's mouth, but his mind was already racing ahead. When they turned up with the escaped convict and the boy, he'd be a hero for breaking the case. He could see the headlines now, "Local Police Officer Nabs Notorious Killer and Thwarts His Sinister Plans to Harm a Small Boy." His old man would have to be proud of him then. It'd be first page material for sure.

"Lewinsky, you listening to me?" Mel asked. About half way through telling him he needed to let the agents in on the info, the kid's eyes glazed over, and he got a goofy grin on his face. In all his years in service, he'd never known anyone quite so flighty as Lewinsky. Made him glad he was nearing retirement. If he had to go out on the streets with this nut job, he'd constantly be worried that he'd misplace his head before they got back to the station.

Lewinsky nodded his head absently. It wasn't until he saw Mel sauntering over to the FBI weasels in the doorway that he registered what he'd actually said. If he let those agents in on it, Lewinsky'd lose the glory for sure. The Feds were notorious for breezing in and twisting things so they looked like saints. They always managed to let the local law enforcement do all the work, and they soaked up all the praise.

Before Lewinsky could stop him, he heard Mel filling tweedle dumb and tweedle dee in on what they'd been talking about. From the muddy tracks down to the cabin in the woods, he gave them all the information they'd need to catch Cole. To Mel's credit, he made it known Lewinsky was the one who'd put two and two together. As he sidled up beside him, Mel even suggested that Lewinsky go along to help investigate the lead.

Both FBI men looked from Mel to Lewinsky and back at each other. They burst into laughter and the one on the left said,

"You expect me to believe this know nothing boob saw

some muddy tracks on a rainy night, and we should just automatically assume they have something to do with this investigation?"

The agent smacked his leg and shook his head in amazement. It was more likely that the Pope would turn into an atheist. From everything he'd witnessed from this local yokel, the boy was a major nut job. He ought to be in a padded room rather than out roaming the streets in a police uniform. Heck, if he lived around here, he'd be ashamed to be seen wearing a badge.

Mel shifted his weight to ease the tension on his hip and let the agents laugh it up. He held up his hand to Lewinsky to keep him from clobbering the one who'd opened his mouth. As much as he disliked Lewinsky, these agents had no call dismissing any leads in this investigation, regardless of who they came from. As soon as they appeared to calm down a bit, Mel informed them, "Seems to me like you agents ought to be willing to check out anything at this point. Especially since you've got one of your own laying in the body count this convict has left. How about you radio to the man in charge and see what he thinks?"

His gruff tone made the agent on the right narrow his eyes. He didn't need some old man to tell him what his job ought to be. The geezer looked like he should have hit the retirement home several years ago. Obviously, his own superiors didn't think much of him or they wouldn't have partnered him with the oversized idiot. If he bothered the agent in charge with information from these two, he'd likely lose his job.

"Why don't you hill-billies just go back and sit down? We haven't got time to be entertaining your fairy tales. Never fails. We get sent out to podunk USA and there's always some flat foot thinks he knows the best way to handle things. You'd be best to leave things to the big dogs and just mute yourselves."

His partner nodded his ascent and both abruptly turned so their backs were to the kitchen. Arms crossed, they just assumed the conversation was over. Mel was tempted to unleash Lewinsky on them. Talk about a bunch of pencil pushing pricks. No wonder Cole managed to escape in the first place. If the undercover agent at the prison acted anything like these two, he'd left himself open to getting his throat slit. The first rule in any investigation was never to assume any lead shouldn't be followed. Especially since a child's life hung in the balance.

Mel stood with his hands clenched to his sides and gritted his teeth to keep from launching into a tirade. The last thing he wanted was to let fly with the fricker frackers in front of a lady. Granted, Gretchen probably heard her fair share in her day, but he didn't want to contribute.

He was so caught up on his silent fuming, he didn't notice Gretchen until she stood beside him. With her finger pressed to her lips, she motioned for Mel and Lewinsky to follow her. When she had them back out of ear shot, she whispered,

"I'll distract the doublemint twins, and you guys scadaddle out the back. They have their heads so far up their rears, I don't think they'll even notice you're gone. I heard what you said, and I don't want to take any chances. I want my little Caleb back in one piece."

Mel exchanged looks with Lewinsky. He couldn't believe he was willingly following Lewinsky anywhere, but he didn't figure he had much choice. Grabbing his hat off the table, he nodded to Gretchen and motioned Lewinsky to follow him. With any luck, they'd make it out to the patrol car before anyone noticed they'd left the premises.

When they made it off the porch and down the driveway,

Mel sighed with relief. He'd half expected Lewinsky to trip over his own feet and set the whole herd of agents on their tail. At the car, he dug in his pocket and tossed the keys to Lewinsky.

"Just keep it between the ditches kid and give me your cell phone. I want to get a hold of Austin and Terrance. Maybe we can get them to help us check out the cabin, that is, if they aren't still tied up looking for Kristian."

Terrance snapped his seat belt in place and flipped open the cell phone. It seemed rather out of place in his wrinkled hand as he ran the other hand through his white hair. The buttons were so tiny he wasn't sure he could even dial the thing. If he had problems keeping his finger confined to one number at a time, it was a wonder old meaty paws could even use the thing.

Chapter 24

His pocket started singing "Take Me Out to the Ball game," so Austin stepped away from the crowd to answer. Not long after they discovered Kristian, the wayward FBI agents came barreling through the woods. Flashlights blazing, they nearly mowed Royce over. He had his back to them and his flashlight aimed towards Terrance and Austin. Both officers were laying flat on the ground, looking down at Kristian. The agents just assumed he had them at gunpoint and blazed in to take him down. In the dark, the agents claimed, Royce's silhouette looked a lot like Cole Williams. How a hundred pound man with chicken legs looks like a hundred an seventy five pound fugitive was beyond Terrance.

Royce sat nursing his sprained ankle, and Gargarian perched on his lap ready to pounce. His tail twitched in agitation, and he just waited for one of them to get close enough to scratch. When the agents charged Royce, the Persian went into attack mode. Hissing and scratching, he drew some blood before his master was able to calm him down. He'd placed his thumb between the cats eyes and applied a little pressure. Although, his eyes blazed in protest, Gargarian calmed himself from a frenzy to a low growl.

Still perched near the opening of the cave, Terrance was in deep conversation with Jack Baily, the leader of the FBI search party. From what he could gather, the agents had gone to the wrong location when they were first dispatched. Rather than Buzzard's Roost they'd headed over to Buzzard's Crest nearly twenty five minutes in the opposite direction. When they heard the bottle rocket in the distance, they assumed it was gunfire and headed over to check it out.

After they'd gotten that misunderstanding straightened out, Terrance finally unclenched his jaw. He'd already decided the FBI had deserted them, only to show up and injure the man who'd actually found Kristian in all this mess. If he wouldn't have known he still needed to find Caleb, he'd have probably let his fist have the pleasure of meeting the guy's face. His smooth baby face looked like it needed a little rearranging. Guy didn't look like he was much over twenty, and his field experienced seemed to be nil.

Austin interrupted Terrance's musings when he bounded over and latched onto his arm. In the semi-darkness, his face took on an eerie glow. The muted flashlight glow made his eyes hollow out and accented his cheek bones. If Terrance didn't know any better, he'd say the man was possessed. Austin's fingers pressed into his forearm, and he exclaimed, "They have a lead on Caleb, and no one will help them. We have to go, now!"

"They, who? And, where exactly are we going?" Terrance questioned. Austin had already turned and attempted to drag him in the direction of the car. Terrance wasn't about to go anywhere until he knew the whole story. Somehow, it didn't seem right to leave these suited imbeciles in charge of getting Kristian to a hospital. Hell, they couldn't even find Buzzard's Roost, how would they be able to coordinate getting a woman out of an underground cave and into an ambulance?

"Mel just called on Lewinsky's phone. Lewinsky spotted some muddy ruts leading from the highway back into the woods on the outer edge of the preserve. Mel said a deserted cabin lays back up that direction and would make for the perfect hideaway for our man. They tried to get the FBI agents at the house to check it out, and they laughed in their faces."

Terrance ran his hand over his mouth and pinched his lower lip between his fingers. He can't say he'd blame the agents for scoffing at Lewinsky. The kid wasn't exactly the sharpest tool in the shed. If they'd been graced with his bumbling presence for any length of time, they already had enough evidence to condemn him as an idiot.

Austin could feel the wheels turning as Terrance mulled it over and reasoned, "Look, if it were Lewinsky alone, I'd say it was a wild goose chase. But, he's convinced Mel that it's worth checking. Mel may have the body of a grandpa, but he's still got the mind of a true investigator. If he's on board with this, it's gotta be the real thing."

Slowly, Terrance nodded his assent. The man had a point. Besides, if they left it up to the FBI agents, they were never going to find Caleb before it was too late.

Jack stood listening to the exchange between the local officers and said, "Why don't you take some of my men with you? We've got enough people out here to keep the lady safe until the rescue team arrives. If your Lewinsky happens to be on target, you're going to need all the help you can get."

Terrance raised his eyebrow with a new respect for this young agent. Most in his position wouldn't have offered any assistance. Especially knowing that his comrades had already shot it down. Jack wasn't just another cog in the FBI machine. Terrance liked that.

Before Austin or Terrance could respond, Jack motioned for

five of his men to come over. Once he had them all lined up, he issued his orders.

"I want you gentlemen to go along with these officers to check out a lead on the missing boy. While you are with them, you will be under their command. That means you do what you're told and don't ask questions. These men have proven themselves worthy of respect already tonight, and I want you to treat them as you would me. Understand?"

The men nodded their agreement. Even though a question remained on several faces, they were all willing to do as instructed. Jack had never steered them wrong before, so they turned to Terrance for further instructions without protest.

Terrance motioned the men to the side and briefly informed the men what Austin had told him. While he instructed them, Austin stuck his hand out to Jack and simply stated, "Thank you. I appreciate any help we can get."

Jack shook the outstretched hand and nodded. He knew what it was like to be in need of some assistance. When he'd first started with the agency, most mocked him for his age and never wanted to give him a chance. It wasn't until he'd proven himself that the superiors started noticing he had an amazing mind. Tonight, this officer had saved him a major blunder when he'd located the woman. He was still kicking himself for the confusion over the names, and if it weren't for Austin, well, they may have been calling the morgue instead of a rescue team. He owed the man more than just the help he'd offered.

Before he turned to go, Austin knelt down beside the lip of the cave and looked down at the woman he loved. Even in her mangled condition, his breath caught at her beauty. He longed to go down and hold her. Just to touch her cheek or brush the hair from her eyes, would be enough to make her real again. She kept closing her eyes, and he could see her wincing from the pain. Every time her lids slid down, his heart beat faster for fear they wouldn't open. He'd already lost her once tonight, and he didn't have the strength do it again.

As he stared down, her eyes fluttered open and her swollen lips parted in a semi-smile. The ache to touch her was overwhelming, but he knew he needed to go if they were going to have a chance to find Caleb. Since he had her attention, he whispered, "I love you."

She saw more than heard his words and answered in kind, "I love you, too." Her forehead furrowed in pain as her lower lip split. Even through the ache, she never took those green eyes off his face. He could feel her emotion penetrating his soul. She had such trust in him, he just hoped he'd be able to live up to her expectations.

"Honey, Terrance and I are going to go. Royce'll be here if you need anything, and the ambulance ought to be coming anytime."

He couldn't bring himself to say they were headed out to look for Caleb. If she knew they had a solid lead, it might build her up for a fall. Somehow giving her false hope wasn't something he wanted to do right now.

Though he hadn't said a thing about her son, Kristian pleaded, "Bring him back to me, Austin, please."

Austin choked on a sob and brushed a tear from his eye. He nodded slowly, unable to speak and turned to join the others. With any luck, they'd still be able to meet Lewinsky and Mel before they had to do too much waiting. He'd told them to sit tight until they got there. Those two were no match for a ruthless killer.

Chapter 25

Caleb wrinkled his nose and felt the wiggly lines come up in the middle. The very tip of his nose itched, but he couldn't quite get it scratched. His hands were still bound to his feet. When he tried to raise his arms, his legs were pulled up at the ankles. Then, he'd lose his balance and nearly bang into the floor. He was afraid to make any noise. The boogie man had finally gone to sleep, and he didn't want to wake him up.

A shiver went down his spine as he thought about the way the man hit him. His face still tingled where the calloused hand met his jaw. He could feel the raised bumps were his face was pinched between the cracks in his fingers. Tyler didn't say nothing about the boogie man hitting nobody. For the first time, he felt more knowledgeable than his five year old buddy. Just wait till he told him.

Caleb's heart sank, he probably wasn't going to get to tell him. After he got sold away to the bad people, he'd never see Tyler...or his momma. Screwing up his face, Caleb told himself not to cry. Crying is for babies, and he wasn't some snot nosed baby like Karen. Karen was Tyler's baby cousin. All she did was squall and poop her pants. Then when they cleaned her up, she squawked some more. Very much not like him.

Sinking back further against the dusty sofa, Caleb started looking around the cabin. Everything had a layer of dust on it and looked like it needed a good scrubbing. He thought Gretchen would have a fit if she saw all this filth. He grinned when he imagined her with one hand on her hip and the other on a mop. She'd give that floor what for, and it'd be sorry it ever got this dirty in the first place.

As Caleb went to shift positions again, he felt something hard in his back pockets. Rocking back and forth, the rounded metal pressed into his bottom first on one side and then the other. Suddenly, his eyes flew up as he realized what he had. He'd stuck Terrance's handcuffs in his pocket. They were to big to cram into one, so he'd stuck one cuff in each pocket. The chain dangled between and cut into his tail bone.

Biting his lower lip in thought, Caleb tried to figure out what Terrance would do. He said the cuffs were for bad guys. From what he could tell, the boogie man was definitely a bad guy. If he could just figure out how to get himself unhog-tied, he'd be able to clamp it on the man while he slept. He was making enough noise sleeping maybe he wouldn't notice. The boogie man could really snore. His snorting made the floor vibrate.

Rolling his wrists in a circle, Caleb tried to weasel his hands out of his nylon restraints. He twisted and pulled, grunted and strained. After several minutes, the fabric started to loosen around his wrists. Bending down, he hooked his feet on the knot between his hands and pushed. He felt his joint pop and then, sweet freedom. His right hand dislodged first, and he used it to get the other one free.

Caleb rubbed his hands together to try and easy the ache where the hose had been. Since his hands were mobile, he decided to untie his feet. The knot was too snug, and he couldn't squeeze his feet through the holes. The strain hurt his ankles too much, and he let out a low moan.

Instantly, he clapped a hand over his mouth and watched as the boogie man shifted position. The sound interrupted his snoring, and Caleb thought he was waking up for sure. The man smacked his lips a little and then continued his noise making right where he left off.

Caleb exhaled slowly and let the relief flood over him. He wasn't ready to deal with another round with Mr. Hateful. Some adults got frustrated with his questions, but apparently the boogie man had a low tolerance level for curiosity. Not to mention that he had hands of steel that he wasn't afraid to use.

Since his legs were still bound together, Caleb army crawled over towards the hammock. He used his arms to pull and let his legs drag along behind him. His little body made a trail through the grim on the floor as he made his way over.

Once he sat just inches in front of the man, he eyeballed the situation. Cole lay with one arm under his face and the other dangling over the edge of the hammock. Caleb felt certain he could get one cuff on the free arm, but wasn't sure he could cuff the other one. It would require sticking his hand awfully close to the boogie man's mouth. If the man wasn't afraid to deck him, he probably had no qualms biting him. Caleb didn't really want to loose any fingers in the process.

Looking around, he noticed the metal pole holding up the hammock was just close enough he might be able to clasp it. It wouldn't be like in the movies where the bad guys had their hands behind their back, but at least he'd be strapped to something solid.

Caleb reached in his back pocket and pulled the handcuffs around where he could see them. Taking a deep breathe, he silently prayed. *God, make me brave like Woody, Amen.* Slowly, he put the open cuff around the dangling arm. Careful not to touch the hand, he looped it around and began to click it into place. As the teeth pushed through the latch, Caleb winced as it made a loud clacking sound. Fortunately, he managed to get it into place, and the sleeping monster never moved.

Biting his tongue in concentration, he reached to clasp the other end on the bar. The chain between cuffs was too short to reach without pulling against the arm. Caleb muttered, "Dirty darn," under his breath and decided he better make it as quick as possible. If the boogie man woke up before he got the other end secure, he'd knock him around for sure.

When he got nervous, Caleb always sang to himself. He imagined his momma's voice singing "Jesus Loves Me" as he geared up to do the impossible. It was all a matter of timing. He had to jerk the arm and click the cuff onto the metal bar before the beast fully awoke. If he was going to do that, he'd have to be speed fast. When he go to the part that said "for the Bible tells me so," Caleb jerked with all his might.

As the other clasp snapped into place, he heard the boogie man shout, "What the…"

Caleb flopped back on his bottom and flipped over to pull himself back across the floor. He tried to crawl out of reach, but he wasn't fast enough. The hand that was once a pillow for the boogie man snapped out and grabbed him by the ankle. When he latched on, Caleb kicked and knocked him off balance. Cole came crashing down out of the hammock and landed on top of the boy's legs. It wasn't until his wrist snapped against the metal that he realized his other arm was in a set of cuffs.

Still blurry from sleep, Cole couldn't believe what he was seeing. He jerked his trapped arm hard against the pole. Again and again, he pulled trying to free himself. The only thing his flailing did was make his wrist shout with pain. It shot up his arm and made the nerves tingle in his shoulder. Wild eyed, he looked down at the frightened face of his son.

Caleb lay flat on his back, eyes wide open. For once, he was too scared to speak. He clenched his teeth to keep his jaw from trembling and tried not to focus on the pain in his legs. The boogie man still lay across his shins, and when he'd landed, Caleb felt something pop. The white hot ache made it impossible to tell whether it was his ankle or part of his leg that had given way.

Enraged, Cole jerked back onto his knees. His upper body came up and freed Caleb's legs. Before the boy could react, Cole used his free arm to grasp the knot that still held Caleb's feet together. He jerked with all his might, and Caleb came skidding across the floor to him. His tiny head bounced off the floor like popcorn as the force pulled him towards the enemy.

Once he had the boy at close range, Cole wrapped his hand around the white throat. He cupped Caleb's chin in his palm and pressed his fingers into the grove behind his jaw. In one fluid motion, he lifted Caleb up by his head and held him directly in front of his face.

"Do you have any idea who you're messing with, you worthless brat? If you ever want to see your momma again before I end you, you best be giving me the key to these cuffs!"

The menace in his tone hurt far more than the pain in Caleb's jaw. His feet dangled, barely touching the floor. Every time his left foot came into contact with the concrete, a streak of pain shot up and settled in the pit of his stomach. Caleb's heart pounded against his chest. He didn't have any keys to these cuffs. Terrance gave them to Gretchen. He was just the keeper of the handcuffs and nothing more.

Caleb tried to swallow the lump in his throat, but he couldn't force it down past the hand squeezing his neck. He'd never seen anyone look so angry before. Even when Gretchen blew a fuse, he could still tell she loved him underneath all the huff and puff. The boogie man just seemed to have a never ending well of rage that bubbled just below the surface.

"Where is the key?" Cole fumed. He shook Caleb and without giving him time to respond he demanded, "Answer me, you piece of shit. I command you as your father, now give."

His father? That couldn't be right, Caleb thought. His daddy wasn't the boogie man. He'd died when he was a baby from some sort of cancer in his brain. Momma told him so every time he asked why he was the only one who didn't have somebody to call daddy. She'd hugged him close and said he may not have a daddy, but he had an Austin who was better than the real thing anyway. This boogie man not only hit, but he lied, too.

The rage in Cole's face made his cheeks turn red and a vein started bumping in his forehead. Caleb glanced away behind him, afraid to make eye contact. When he did, he couldn't believe what he saw. Standing in the window, was Austin. He held his fingers to his lips, and then held up his hands in the "I love you" symbol.

Caleb had to fight back a smile and his eyes got huge with the secret he couldn't tell. Focusing back on the boogie man, he made out like he was trying to speak. He sputtered and coughed against the hand that was choking off his air supply.

Realizing the boy couldn't respond even if he wanted to, Cole eased his grip on Caleb's throat. He'd have plenty of time to make him pay after he got freed from these handcuffs. Cole was still in shock that a four year old managed to get him strapped to a pole. Where in the hell had he gotten the handcuffs from to begin with? Wasn't like the average brat kept a set in his back pocket or something.

199

As soon as his windpipe was freed, Caleb gasped for a lung full of air. His sides were burning from lack of oxygen, and he felt like he did that time when he'd fallen in the pool swallowing half the water on his way down. When he could get his throat to work, he croaked, "The key is under the sofa."

Caleb clasped his eyelids shut and waited for the lightening to strike. God didn't like it when you told lies. Momma didn't either. But maybe, just maybe, God would let it slide just this once since the boogie man was trying to choke him out. He'd be sure to be extra good next week to make up for it. If he got to see next week, that is.

"The sofa? Why would it be over there?" Cole asked sarcastically. This boy reminded him of his conniving mom. She'd been known to pull one over on him. How was he to know this little brat wasn't doing the same thing?

"I…put it there when you had me all tied up. I didn't want you to take it out of my pocket once I had you all cuffed up."

Sounded logical, Cole thought. Just to be sure, he figured he'd better inspect the boy's pockets himself. Laying a leg over the boys knees, he used his free hand to explore Caleb's pockets. He roughly jabbed his first two fingers into each pocket and patted down his shirt. The only thing he came up with was a rubber band and a piece of fuzz.

Cole debated whether to let the boy go out of his reach or not. Once he got by the sofa, whose to say he'd actually bring the key back over to him. But, then again, it wasn't like he had much choice. He couldn't stay strapped here forever, and the metal pole wasn't going to budge anytime soon. He'd just have to light the boy's butt on fire with fear. Fear for himself and fear for his worthless momma ought to bring him marching back with the key.

"Tell you what. You go get that key for me, and I'll pretend this little altercation didn't happen."

Cole narrowed his eyes and leaned into to where his breath caressed Caleb's face. He leered at him as he noticed the blue mark on his jaw. He'd connected pretty good earlier when the brat wouldn't shut his trap. Taking his thumb, Cole pressed it into the tender bruise and snorted,

"You get over there and get any ideas about not bringing it back, I'll kill you. Slow and painful. Not only that, but I'll take you to your momma's makeshift grave and let her watch as I squeeze the life out of you. Then when I'm done, I'll end your momma too. Do I make myself clear?"

Caleb nodded his ascent vigorously. Golly, here he was lying again. He couldn't exactly bring back a key that didn't even exist. Tears welled up in his eyes, and now his momma was going to suffer over his fib, too. Silently, he prayed God would help Austin save him before he had to turn up with the key.

When the boogie man finally released him, Caleb rubbed his hand across his face. The tender skin throbbed where the thumb pressed against it. Taking his time, Caleb turned and shimmied slowly across the floor. His left leg hurt something fierce and the pantyhose knot keeping jerking against it as he moved. Each time he pulled himself up to move, pain raced up his leg making it hard to motivate.

Inch by inch, he made his way across the floor until he lay flat in front of the sofa. His breath came in labored gasps as he realized he was now officially done for. He wouldn't be able to produce the key and then he'd never see his momma. *Please God, let momma forgive me. I'm sorry,* he inwardly prayed.

As he reached his hand under the sofa to buy some time, he heard a loud thud. The cool damp air rushed in as the door exploded inward. Instantly, the foot that protruded through the door materialized into Austin. In filed Terrance and several other men Caleb had never seen before. The little boy was never so happy to see someone in his whole life. Despite the pain, his face spread into a cockeyed grin. Momma was right, he did have an Austin and he was the best thing going.

Caleb lay on the floor and watched as the men wrestled the boogie man into another set of cuffs. It took all of them to contain him since he fought like a polecat. Arm flying one way, he used his legs to pull the officers down whenever they tried to get close. His rage had gone out of control, and it was like fighting someone consumed by the devil. Finally, Austin clobbered him on the base of the skull, and he fell unconscious. While he was out, they pinned his arms behind his back and shackled his ankles together.

Once the beast was contained, Austin turned to check on Caleb. His heart ached to see the mark on his face, and he rushed over to hold him. He scooped him up onto his lap. As he did, the boys leg brushed against the sofa, and he yelped in pain.

"Are you okay?" Austin asked anxiously. He hadn't expected him to cry out when he picked him up.

Caleb nestled into his chest and buried his face in his neck. With both arms wrapped around Austin's shoulders, he said, "Yuh, huh. But, my leg really hurts."

"We'll get ya checked out here in a minute."

Austin was too choked up to say anymore. He snuggled his face down into Caleb's hair and took in that little boy smell. Caleb's heart thumped against his chest, and Austin could feel his trying to stay in rhythm. He sent a silent word of thanks to God for keeping his boy safe.

After he'd given the two a moment to reunite, Terrance came over and knelt down in front of Caleb. His little eyes turned to take him in, but he didn't make any move to separate himself from Austin. He'd found his comfort zone and wasn't about to budge.

"Hey, buddy, I was just wondering. Did my handcuffs pass the bad guy test?" Terrance tried to sound serious, but grinned as he asked the question.

Caleb's head shot up off Austin's shoulder, and his eyes danced with eagerness.

"Yes, sirree. They held up real good against the boogie man. Thanks for loaning um' to me. They came in mighty handy."

Boogie man? Terrance raised an eyebrow at the reference and gave Austin a look. He ruffled the boy's hair with his hand and told him, "I'm real proud of you for thinking to use them. Just how, exactly, did you get him to hold still while you strapped him down. Why it took seven grown men to cuff him when we got here. What did you do, put him in a sleeper hold?"

Forgetting his pain, Caleb warmed up to the subject and eagerly replied, "Nope. But he was sleepin'. He started making this loud noise like a buzz saw, you know? And well, I just weaseled out of the pantyhose he had around my hands and crawled right up to him, like an army guy. Then, I thunk about it real hard and was real careful and put one cuff on his arm that was dangling down. And, um, then the cuff wasn't long enough to reach, and I pulled real fast to snap it on to the pole. That's where I messed it up, 'cause then he waked up and flopped on top of me. I think I heard my leg broked when he landed on me. The boogie man, he's real heavy, you know, and well, it really hurted."

Caleb stuck his lip out for emphasis and shook his head at his own mistake. Austin leaned around to where he could look the boy in the face and told him proudly, "You done good, son, real good. It was brave to do what you did and I'm proud of you."

The pout turned into a cockeyed grin, but it only lasted an instant. When Austin said he did good, he didn't know the whole story. He hadn't told him about the part where he lied to the boogie man. Even if it was just the boogie man, God probably still wasn't real happy with him. Maybe if he told Austin, he could have talk with God so he wouldn't be so mad at him.

"Austin, I done something bad. REAL bad." The solemn voice made Terrance and Austin look at each other. The child sounded like he'd just committed hairy carey or something.

"It's okay, little man. Whatever it is, you can tell me."

"'Member when I seed you in the window, and you do'd like this?" Caleb held his finger up to his mouth. "Well, I told the boogie man a lie. I know I'm not supposed to, and it makes God sad and all, but…I did it. I tell'd him I hid the key to the handcuffs under the sofa so'd he'd let me get away from him. I just wanted him to stop hurting me."

"Oh, Caleb, you don't need to feel bad about that. God understands that sometimes you have to bend the truth a little when you're trying to get away from a bad man. If you hadn't done what you did, we'd never have been able to get in here to save you."

Caleb took in what Austin said and scrunched up his forehead in thought. So, telling a lie was okay if you told it to a bad guy. He guessed that made sense but before he could totally relax he asked, "We don't have to tell Momma, do we? She may not be aware of the lying rules when your talking to bad guys. I don't feel up to a spankin' right now."

The serious look on his face made Austin laugh. Somehow, he was pretty certain the last thing she was going to do when she saw Caleb was spank him.

"Don't worry, we'll keep it just between us boys. Come on, little man, let's get you to a hospital to check out that leg."

Caleb gave him a toothy smile and snuggled back against his

chest. The rough fabric aggravated his bruised cheek, but he didn't care. He was just glad his Austin had come to save him from the bad man. And, it didn't hurt that he was willing to keep his secret either.

Chapter 26

Kristian sat on her front porch swing with her foot propped up on a wicker table. Her leg was still in a cast, but her face was finally starting to heal. She'd definitely have a scar, but at least the pain was easing, inside and out.

Her husband sat next to her, watching as their son hobbled around on his crutches. Even in a cast, the insufferable Caleb still flit around with ants in his pants and a question on his lips. He seemed to be recovering from his ordeal rather well. Aside from the occasional nightmare, he was going to be as good as new.

Kristian sat down her coffee cup and lay her head on Austin's shoulder. He leaned his cheek against her hair and felt her warm breath on his neck. Ever since the night he nearly lost her, he couldn't bear to have her out of his sight. While she still lay in the hospital bed, he had a minister marry them. They'd already seen the worst. Now, all they had to look forward to was the better.

Printed in the United States
59511LVS00002B/445-519

9 781424 143887